I0708904

OF RETREATS AND REVENGE

PHILLIPA NEFRI CLARK

Storm

This is a work of fiction. Names, characters, businesses, places, events and incidents are either the products of the author's imagination or used in a fictitious manner. Any resemblance to actual persons, living or dead, or actual events is purely coincidental.

Copyright © Phillipa Nefri Clark, 2021, 2026

The moral right of the author has been asserted.

Previously published in 2021 as *Tales of Life and Daph: Have Camper, Will Marry*.

All rights reserved. No part of this book may be reproduced or used in any manner without the prior written permission of the copyright owner. This prohibition includes, but is not limited to, any reproduction or use for the purpose of training artificial intelligence technologies or systems.

To request permissions, contact the publisher at rights@stormpublishing.co

Ebook ISBN: 978-1-83700-094-4
Paperback ISBN: 978-1-83700-095-1

Cover design: Diane Meacham
Cover images: Shutterstock

Published by Storm Publishing.
For further information, visit:
www.stormpublishing.co

ALSO BY PHILLIPA NEFRI CLARK

Temple River

The Cottage at Whisper Lake

The Bookstore at Rivers End

The House at Angel's Beach

The Secrets of Willow Bay

The Lost Girl of Seahaven

A Travelling Celebrant Mystery

Of Marriage and Murder

Of Funerals and Feuds

Of Vines and Victims

Rivers End Romantic Women's Fiction

The Stationmaster's Cottage

Jasmine Sea

The Secrets of Palmerston House

The Christmas Key

Taming the Wind

Martha

Detective Liz Moorland Series

Lest We Forgive

Lest Bridges Burn

Lest Tides Turn

Lest Nobody Lives

Lest Angels Weep

Last Known Contact

Charlotte Dean Mysteries
Christmas Crime in Kingfisher Falls
Book Club Murder in Kingfisher Falls
Cold Case Murder in Kingfisher Falls
Plans for Murder in Kingfisher Falls
Festive Felony in Kingfisher Falls

Bindarra Creek Rural Fiction
A Perfect Danger
Tangled by Tinsel

Doctor Grok's Peculiar Shop Short Story Collection
Simple Words for Troubled Times

ONE

WHAT HAPPENS IN THE
GARDEN, STAYS IN THE GARDEN

If it wasn't for the mysterious note, Daphne would be asleep by now, enjoying the rare luxury of silk sheets and a whole king-size four poster bed to herself. She might have left the French doors open to the balcony to let the warm night air in. Or she might have closed the doors and slept with only a sheet covering her night wear. The choice was hers.

If it wasn't for the mysterious note, she'd have read more of the paperback she'd begun as she enjoyed a late evening cup of tea. Or she might have indulged in a spa bath before donning the hotel dressing gown and writing notes about the people she'd met that day to share with John tomorrow. More choices she'd have enjoyed making.

But there *was* a note which left *choice* out of the equation!

Daphne stopped near the dark, deserted tennis courts and checked the note in question using the flashlight on her phone.

There was a map—hand-drawn squiggles which represented the hotel and its outer buildings, along with a couple of paths. If she was reading this right, she needed to head to the English garden behind the high hedges.

A shiver ran up her spine to her neck and the tiny hairs stood up. Turning off the flashlight, she gazed around. Was there someone in the shadows, watching her? More likely the tingle of fear was a response to her solitary venture.

Alone in the dark in a strange place. Good one, Daph.

But by the time she'd seen the envelope on the floor slipped beneath the door to her suite, the hotel was quiet. It was past midnight and her gentle tap on the door of the next suite got no response. She didn't know which rooms belonged to anyone else she'd met during the evening and the reception desk had a 'back at six a.m.' sign on it.

Had her neighbour been awake, she would have had someone to show the note to. Get another opinion. And possibly some company on this trek through the grounds of a secluded hotel. But he wasn't.

When nothing moved around her, she turned the flashlight back on and drew a deep breath. Above the map were handwritten instructions and it was those which had compelled her to put on sensible shoes and let herself out of the hotel at this hour.

Come to the fountain at the top of the mountain.

It was the first line in a poem of sorts.

The rest of it was about singing and dancing in the dark and more invitation to meet. And seeing who had left the hotel a few minutes ago left her no option but to follow.

"Next time don't look out of the window," she muttered, raised the flashlight to light her way, and got going again.

Between the high, perfectly manicured hedges was an archway of climbing roses leading into the English garden. Daphne hesitated, peering into the gloom. Above her, heavy clouds scudded along, threatening rain. She flashed the light around and squealed as a figure loomed close by.

Get a grip, Daph. It's a statue!

Now her heart was thudding. This was a terrible idea. Out here so far from the hotel in the dead of night. It was time to go back before she scared herself again.

But she couldn't. Not until she located the note writer.

She forced her feet to cross the grass to the five-tiered fountain.

All was quiet.

"Well, that is odd."

The fountain wasn't splashing. No water flowed. Did the staff turn it off at night?

As she reached the fountain the clouds parted, and moonlight streamed onto the garden highlighting the statues and benches. The garden beds.

And the body face down in the water.

A body wearing a red velvet jacket.

TWO
A LITTLE BIT PERFECT

Earlier that weekend

"Two nights in a luxury queen suite with valley views. All meals including sumptuous breakfasts and the gala dinner. Champagne on arrival. Heated pool. Spa treatments by appointment. Oh my, John, pinch me!"

Daphne Jones didn't mean the last bit, but she couldn't stop smiling. She and John had rarely stayed in a hotel let alone a five-star exclusive retreat in the mountains, but this is exactly where they were heading. This very minute. Or they would be once John was finished settling Bluebell and the SUV in at the secure carpark partway up the mountain. A dozen or more cars were already here but not another soul in sight, except for the driver of the 4WD who waited near his vehicle.

"Have you got everything, Daph? Nothing left inside you'll need because once we're up there, we can't duck back down at will."

"I'll check again. Just in case."

She climbed into their caravan and headed first to the

bedroom. The bed was neatly made, ready for their return. The narrow side tables on either side were clear of everything other than the paperback she'd read for a few minutes earlier and she reached for it before pulling back her hand.

"Silly idea. No time for reading!"

Nothing of importance remained in the bathroom. Her makeup bag was already in her suitcase in the 4WD. So was John's shaver and her hair dryer. Probably a five-star hotel would have hair dryers but better to be safe than sorry.

She checked the rest of Bluebell and ended up in the kitchen, frowning at one of those annoying nagging feelings she'd forgotten something.

"Ready, doll?" John called.

"Be right there."

When I remember.

It was something important. Something to share...

"Dandelions and ducks!" She opened the small pantry and pulled out two containers. "Fancy leaving you behind."

John stuck his head in with a smile. Then he saw what Daphne carried and it disappeared.

"Are you sure you want to take them? There'll be plenty to eat there."

She passed him the containers. "They're not just food. They are for making friends with. Everyone loves cookies."

"You might offend the chef bringing your own supplies."

"I'll make sure the chef gets first bite then. One can make friends with more than the other guests."

John sighed. She was sure it was a sigh. But he nodded and carried the containers to the 4WD and found space in his duffel bag for them. She closed Bluebell's door and locked it, then ran a hand over the bright blue and white exterior. "We won't be long. You have a nice rest."

The driver glanced at his watch and she got the message. The poor man had been there for an hour and probably wanted a cup of tea. Perhaps a cookie might help? But John opened the door for her.

It took her a minute to work out the best way to get in. Her right foot on the running plate didn't let her get traction so she switched legs, reached up for the handle on the inside, and pulled. John gave her a little push and she was in. Much higher than their SUV. John got in from the other side and they put on their seatbelts as the driver hoisted himself up with more style than they'd shown.

"I'm Colin. Col. The road up the mountain is narrow and a bit winding in spots but it'll give you some decent views. If either of you feel car sick give me plenty of notice. Can't always stop and I'd rather not have to clean up after you. Apart from that, sit back and enjoy the trip. Be there in about twenty minutes."

Colin was a solid man in his forties. He wore tan shorts and shirt with the hotel logo on a pocket and had dark sunglasses on a broad, stubbled face.

As they pulled out of the fenced carpark, a similar 4WD approached and Colin raised his hand as they passed.

"That's my wife. Cherry. She'll bring the next couple up."

Daphne glanced behind as the 4WD nosed onto a dirt road. Bluebell and their car, along with the vehicles of the other guests, would be locked in at nighttime. Not that it was likely any car thieves would venture to this remote spot but one never knew. Another car drove in. It must be a procession of 4WD's up and down to the hotel because nobody was permitted to use the road other than the staff of the resort and every guest was ferried there by one of these vehicles.

"Don't remember seeing you folk before. First visit?" Col had to raise his voice over the motor as he navigated onto another road, this one even narrower than the last.

"Yes! I'm here for the Celebrating Celebrants conference."

The invitation to attend had surprised Daphne. And baffled her. She'd been a registered celebrant for more than a year but only recently retired from the real estate agency she and John owned and had operated for decades in their hometown of Rivers End.

Being on the road with Bluebell gave her the freedom to accept more appointments and she was almost booked out for several months ahead.

"I wonder why they've invited me?" she'd asked John at the time. "It says there are only fifty invites and I'd have thought I'd be a long way down the list."

Well, I'm here now and cannot wait to get started!

The invitation included free access to every aspect of the conference including the gala dinner and a discounted accommodation and meals package. The latter was to be paid for on arrival and Daphne had dug into her savings for this lovely little holiday.

Col glanced into his rear-view mirror at John.

"You going out to the river? Saw you have some decent fishing rods back there."

John leaned forward. "I've signed up for a fishing trip. Staying out overnight."

"You'll love it. Best fishing in the state, if you ask me."

As the men continued their discussion about fishing and rivers, Daphne peered through the window. They were climbing up a steep part of the road and every so often a break in the trees to her left offered an enticing flash of the landscape below.

This morning they'd departed from a town more than four hours' drive away after dawn and it was now early afternoon. Along the way they'd stopped for an early lunch and a bit of a wander around an old gold mining town. It was one of the best parts of her new career as an officiant, seeing firsthand the beautiful countryside and quaint towns in her home state of Victoria. The terrain changed constantly and she never tired of the variety.

The past two hours of the trip was across flat land with little to see but endless paddocks and distant hills. As they got closer, those hills became a mountain range which rose high above the plains. And now, here they were following a winding and steep road surrounded by native trees and bushland.

She took her phone out to take some photos.

"Reception is hit and miss up here," Col said. "There's a couple of spots that work most of the time, but don't expect too much."

Sounds perfect.

No phone. No emails. No cooking. No cleaning.

And no murders!

The 4WD bounced around too much to get a clear photo so she put the phone away and drew out the invitation to read again. She still wasn't certain why she'd been invited. According to the information on the association's website, the annual event was open to celebrants in Victoria who'd been full members for five years or more, which Daphne hadn't been. In addition, a handful of new celebrants were invited who'd been recommended by one of their clients.

I wonder who?

There was nothing on the invitation to indicate this. Her first clients were Christie and Martin in Rivers End and then she and John were busy with the real estate agency for some months, so she'd only officiated at a couple of weddings until they hit the road with Bluebell. Nobody stood out.

Of course, some of the ceremonies stood out, but for all the wrong reasons.

Family feuds. Rivalries. Murders.

Surely nobody involved in those events would recommend Daphne, who'd been at the centre of them and unintentionally ruffled feathers with her own brand of sleuthing.

There was a jolt and the 4WD swayed as its wheels on her side sprayed a cloud of dust.

"Sorry. Keep asking for that bit of road to get some attention. The minute there's rain it deteriorates, and the sides are getting soft. But we're almost there." Col had both hands tightly on the steering wheel.

They slowed down to take a hairpin bend and the vista below opened up through a gap in the trees. With a small gasp, she grabbed the handle in the door. This was so high up! With the twists and turns, it hadn't been obvious how much they were climbing but beneath them the plains reached to the horizon, where a heat haze blurred the meeting of land and sky. A small town below was like a toy village. No wonder they'd had to leave Bluebell and their car behind.

A moment later, the road flattened out and widened and Col nosed through a narrower entrance with heavy metal gates on either side and what appeared to be some kind of security system. On one side a discreet sign read 'Hearthstone High Country Retreat'.

Bushland and dust gave way to an open lawn dotted with shaped bushes. They followed a long, paved driveway with graceful weeping birches on either side which led to a building. A two-storey reddish-brown brick building.

I'm transported to Bridgerton!

"Welcome to Hearthstone." Col pulled up outside the double doors. "Hope you like things a bit fancy. This was built to include the best of several styles with optimum comfort."

A woman wearing a formal black suit and bowtie opened the door on Daphne's side. "Mrs Jones? We're so happy to see you." She offered a hand, and Daphne took it to help herself climb down. "Your luggage will be taken to your suite, so please follow me to reception."

John appeared from the back of the vehicle.

"Mr Jones. Please. This way."

The woman headed for the double doors.

Col opened the back of the 4WD as a young man, also in black, pushed a trolley over. "We'll get this up to you."

"Thank you for the lift, Col," John said.

"Pleasure. Enjoy the stay."

John looped Daphne's arm through his. "Ready, doll?"

She gazed up at the building. Close up, the hotel was less like the house in Bridgerton than her first impression. There were large windows and balconies on the upper floor.

"I hope so! This is very fancy."

Even a bit intimidating in its formality.

The woman who'd greeted them held the door open with a smile.

Daphne didn't need a second invitation.

The foyer of the hotel was a throwback to a distant era—and one from another part of the world. A patterned, highly polished timber floor. Enormous, sparkling chandeliers. A sweeping staircase to a mezzanine level. Scattered armchairs. And a marble reception counter where the concierge left them.

No other patrons were in the foyer.

Maybe we stepped back in time!

"Mr and Mrs Jones? I'm Mandy and am so happy to welcome you both." A young woman with flawless makeup and brown hair slicked into a tight bun smiled from across the counter. She also wore a black suit with the logo on a pocket. "Was the ride up the hill comfortable?"

Hill was an understatement.

John nodded. "Col was an excellent driver, thank you."

"What an impressive building!" Daphne gazed around, noticing huge oil paintings on the walls.

"We like it. The current owners are a husband and wife who both love different eras and when they couldn't agree on which one to build, came up with a rather fun combination which is full of luxury."

"Not at all what you expect hidden away up here," Daphne said.

"Your suite has a welcome pack inside which includes information about the grounds, different activities, room service menu should you decide to order in, and complimentary vouchers for the day spa and the fishing trip."

"Complimentary?" This didn't make sense. "I understood those were extras to pay for on arrival, along with the accommodation." She opened her handbag. "I have my credit card—"

Mandy smiled. "No need. They've been taken care of. There

are no hidden charges and nothing to do now other than enjoy your time with us."

"But... who?"

"I'm afraid I can't help with that information." Mandy handed over two keys. "Your suite is on the upper floor, number seventy-six. Behind the staircase you'll find the elevator and when you alight, turn right, and follow the signs. If there is anything at all I can help with, dial seven on the phone in the suite."

Free?

John accepted the keys. "Thank you, Mandy. Do you happen to know when Daphne is expected for the conference? We didn't get much information."

"There is an itinerary in the suite. Officially the conference begins in the morning, but a number of patrons are already here and out enjoying the grounds or a spa treatment. I believe there is a meet and greet in the bar later."

The phone rang and Mandy excused herself.

As they waited for the elevator, John kissed her cheek. "Someone is very generous."

"Oh my, they certainly are. And I shall make sure I pay it forward."

"Always kind-hearted. Well, here's the lift. Shall we go and see what's in store for us?" John asked as the doors opened.

She nodded but her mind was racing. What had she possibly done to deserve this?

THREE

A ROOM WITH MANY VIEWS

John used his key to open door seventy-six and pushed it wide to let Daphne go in first. She'd been quiet on the short ride in the elevator and not commented when the doors opened to a spacious lounge area with another chandelier and its own balcony.

Are you worrying about who paid for this?

It was a surprise. When the invitation arrived some weeks ago, there was accompanying information about the cost, and it wasn't an inexpensive weekend. Daphne, though, was determined to pay for it from the money she'd saved over the past few months. In the past he'd always paid for everything. They were an old-fashioned couple that way and it came from John's desire to never put Daphne in a position of feeling money was an issue, like she had growing up. Goodness knows she'd contributed equally over their marriage and although he was better with money, she was better with people and making their clients return time and again.

He closed the door in his wake and followed her down a short hall. As the space opened up, he found himself smiling.

"Would you look at this?"

They'd rarely gone far from home in the past. The occasional visit to the city was about as far as they'd travelled until Bluebell came along. But this room... this suite, was amazing.

It was situated on a corner of the building and the main living area was as big as Bluebell's total size. A small dining table was near a discreet counter with a fridge, kettle, and coffee machine. Then a sofa and two armchairs with coffee tables nestled close to a well-stocked bookcase. Finally, a couple of tub style chairs faced an expansive window looking over the trees back to where they'd driven from today. A spectacular view.

"Love, come in here!" Daphne called from another room.

This was the bedroom, and it wasn't the four-poster bed that had Daphne excited, nor the day sofa, and not even what looked like a decadent bathroom, but the balcony.

John stepped through French doors onto decorative tiles. The outlook was to the front of the hotel, over the gardens of the estate from the driveway across to tennis courts, a croquet lawn, and a swimming pool. Beyond those, the bushland returned, and the peak of the mountain towered above them.

"Imagine this in winter!"

"You are so excited, Daph. And it would be incredible to see all this with a blanket of snow but I'm pleased it is summer."

Daphne leaned against him. "Bet you can't wait to get going."

"For once I'd like to be in two places at one time." He chuckled and put an arm around Daphne. "I can hear the river calling but would be just as happy to wander around here and have dinner with you."

She went quiet again. They were rarely apart, and he couldn't remember the last time they'd not slept in the same bed.

"If you'd rather I stay—"

"Don't be silly!" Daphne dug him in the ribs with her elbow. Lightly. "I'm perfectly alright here for one night and will be busy. And I want you to have the best fishing trip ever, love. I mean it."

Another 4WD rattled along the driveway, stopping much where Col had a little earlier. Three people climbed out as well as the driver. Three women, and when the concierge walked across, they all greeted her as if old friends.

"Not first timers, I'd say," Daphne commented. "I'm getting nervous about meeting all these established officiants."

He took her hand and they wandered inside, back to the living room. "You will charm them all by being yourself. When would you like to go back downstairs? I see all our luggage is already here. Except my rods."

"Perhaps if we take a look at the itinerary... oh, I didn't see that!" Daphne dashed across to the dining table where a bottle of champagne was in an ice bucket. There were two glasses and a basket with chocolates and fruit. "I have an idea. Rather than open it today when you are going to be hiking soon, what if it goes into the fridge and we'll have a glass when you get back?"

"Good thinking. And speaking of me heading off, I might change into my hiking clothes if you don't mind."

Daphne was busy putting the bottle into the fridge. "Don't mind one bit. I'm going to take a look at the information pack here."

At least she was back to her normal self. He'd been serious about staying with her if she was uncomfortable being on her own for a night. But Daph was treating this like an adventure. And she'd have a wonderful time.

Once John returned to the bedroom, Daphne rested her hands on the back of a dining chair and released a long breath in a whoosh. Everything here was perfect and she couldn't wait to explore outside and meet the other attendees. But still...

If only I knew why this is free.

She pulled the chair out and sat, opening a folder titled 'Hearthstone High Country Retreat Welcome Packet.'

There was a map of the hotel. One elevator. Two floors plus an entertainment area on the roof beside the restaurant. Most of the accommodation was on their level with the exception of the manager's quarters on the lower floor. Also on the bottom floor was the conference room, a bar, and café.

A second map covered the expansive grounds. Backing onto

the bushland behind the hotel was the general staff quarters and garages for the vehicles. As they'd seen from the balcony there were several areas for recreation. Close to the main building was the standalone day spa and what a lovely selection of treatments were on offer. Massages, hairdressing, makeup, and more... personal treatments. There was a recommendation to book as soon as possible to ensure an appointment but she would wait until John headed off.

Next was the itinerary of the conference. The first session began at ten in the morning. There was an invitation to attend a 'meet and greet' at the bar at six today which seemed a good idea. At this point, she knew nobody except by names she'd seen thanks to the association's website. Afterwards, she had options of a table in the restaurant or ordering room service. Something to decide later.

"I'm ready, Daph. And had a text message from reception to say we leave in half an hour." John joined her at the table. "Looks like a lot of reading there."

She smiled. "Do you have any idea of how busy I'm going to be? Once you leave, I'll book something nice at the day spa. I want to go for a walk around the grounds and then be back here to change for the meet-up at the bar downstairs at six. I hope they like me."

John covered her hand with his. "No self-doubt. Okay? Meeting new people is your thing. Think of them as potential clients and you'll be in your element."

He was right. People were her passion, and it wasn't as if she had to deal with feuding families or missing bodies. This was a fun event and she would enjoy every second. A little bubble of excitement had her tapping her toes beneath the table.

"And what about tomorrow?" he asked.

"I might have breakfast on the balcony. And then there is a full day of sessions. You'll be back late afternoon?"

He nodded. "Far as I know we have an hour of hiking each way and the camping area is already set up, so straight into fishing. We cook what we catch and any excess goes into a portable fridge to bring back. Once I'm back I'll be diving straight into the shower to offload all the fishy and river smell and into my suit and then we, my sweetheart, will have a ball at the gala dinner."

"Which reminds me, I need to get my clothes hung up in case any need pressing. Can't get all dressed up for a ball and have creases in my skirt." She stood. "Do you know what your accommodation is like?"

"Only that it is a tent. But no idea how big or small so might be a nostalgic trip to those occasional weekends when I headed into the Otway Ranges to fish." John laughed as he got to his feet. "I might return tomorrow with bags under my eyes from no sleep from laying on the ground after forgetting how to make a camp bed."

"I have faith in you, love. You are good with your hands."

Those hands were suddenly on either side of her face, gently lifting her chin so he could kiss her lips. Her heart pitter-pattered and she closed her eyes. If he kept this up, he'd be late for his departure. But then he released her and when she flickered her lids open, he was smiling.

"I'd better get going. Need to check my fishing gear is down there seeing as it isn't here."

"Want me to walk you down?"

"You go and unpack. That way, you can start your adventure as well." John kissed her nose. "Have fun. And no sleuthing."

"No sleuthing at all. As long as there are no murders."

He gave her one of those 'don't even go there' looks.

"The only investigating I intend on is checking the menu and finding out what the gossip is," she said.

John groaned and she burst into peals of laughter.

Daphne waved to John from the balcony. He waved back after putting a handful of fishing gear down. A small group was gathered. All were men and most looked to be around John's age. Each carried their own fishing equipment and backpacks. This was a meeting of sorts, perhaps a pre-hike chat about processes, and one man held court. He was thirty or so with shoulder-length hair and a muscular build. Beside him, another man ticked items off a clipboard. Both of these men wore the same style of tan shorts and shirt Col had.

John pulled his floppy white hat from a pocket and after winking at Daphne, put it on his head. A moment later the group was walking away, off in the direction of the tennis courts. John glanced back and she blew him a kiss.

How strange to watch him leave, knowing she'd be on her own until this time tomorrow.

Not alone, Daph. There are forty-nine other celebrants to meet.

He was out of sight.

A little piece of her went with him.

"Have fun, love," she whispered. "Stay safe."

A breeze ruffled her hair, and she wrinkled her nose as smoke wafted from somewhere. Almost like cigarette smoke.

"Do you expect him to fall into the river?"

Daphne spun around. Was someone in the suite?

FOUR

A PECULIAR THING

"Over here, buttercup," the voice continued with a deep chuckle. "I'm beside you, not behind you."

What on earth?

A trail of wispy smoke bridged the gap to the next balcony where a man leaned against the railing, smoking. He was at least seventy, white hair pulled back in a short ponytail and wearing a long white dressing gown with the hotel logo blazoned on the left. He grinned as she looked him up and down.

"Isn't the hotel a smoke free zone?" She spoke before she had a chance to filter the words. Confronting anyone wasn't her thing but he'd given her a small scare and her heart was only just settling down to a normal beat.

"Probably."

She didn't have a response. Not one he'd appreciate. And what had he meant about her expecting John to fall in the river?

"Anyway. It is just a cigar. A rather expensive one and I *am* outside."

A cigar. Her father—her stepfather—used to smoke them on occasion, when he had a raise at work or his football team won something. Not her biological father, who she'd only recently met for the first time, but the man who'd raised her. A man long gone.

"I doubt John will fall in the river. He is a careful man. To answer your question."

The man sucked on the cigar and blew smoke in the opposite direction. There wasn't much left of it and he stubbed it in a small personal ashtray, dropped the remains in, and closed it. "Then why worry about him?"

It was none of his business.

"We are rarely apart."

Good work, Daph. None of his business!

"You are so sweet. No wonder your clients adore you enough to have written the winning nomination."

"The winning... I'm sorry. Who are you?"

The man bowed. "Rupert Witherspoon."

"Oh. But you're the..."

He smiled. "President? I am indeed. And you are Daphne Jones. Known for beautiful weddings, heartfelt funerals, and a spot of sleuthing."

How to respond was taken out of her hands as a beeping sound emanated from his dressing gown pocket. He pulled out a phone. "Time for my medication. Shall I keep a seat for you at the bar?"

"I, er..."

Rupert winked and disappeared into his suite, leaving nothing but the faint remains of his cigar smoke.

Rather than inhale any more of the toxic air, she stepped inside and closed the French door behind herself, perhaps with a little more force than intended. What a peculiar man Rupert was. She'd seen his name on the association newsletters and the like but never a photo.

"Eccentric or just strange?" she muttered. "Buttercup! I'm no buttercup."

Rupert had been reminded to take his medication. Might be to improve his manners?

A smile came to her face, and she chuckled as she collected her handbag. Time she had a look around.

. . .

There were more people checking in as Daphne made her way through the foyer and a couple of the seats were occupied with chatting visitors. Outside, another 4WD with guests pulled up. It wouldn't be long before she'd get to meet some of the other celebrants. But for now, she had plans to wander around the grounds.

The driveway was circular and a path forked away with a small sign to the day spa. Until last year, Daphne had rarely bothered with facials and the like. She had her own regime and looked after herself, or so she'd thought. But then her friend Christie opened a beauty salon in Rivers End and insisted Daphne enjoy some free treatments. After one, she was hooked. Who knew how relaxing a facial was? Or a full body massage.

Being on the road gave fewer opportunities although visiting a hairdresser was one indulgence she did keep. She was fine doing her own skincare and makeup but not keeping the greys away and managing the flash of colour she liked in her brown curls. Her hand went to her head. Not curls so much these days. Christie had shown her how to straighten her hair a certain way which made it shine and feel soft and that was now her preferred style.

The building housing the day spa was like a mini version of the hotel, with the same brickwork and a blackboard near the door with specials. In Daphne's handbag were three vouchers for free services. Any services.

As she stood reading, a door opened and a woman with a cheery face emerged. She wore a white uniform and had lots of black hair escaping from a bun on top of her head.

"Hello there! Would you care to make an appointment? I'm Maisie and I run the spa."

"Oh, yes please. I'm Daphne."

Stepping out to hold the door open, Maisie gestured. "Please, come in and we can find the perfect treatment for you."

Inside was a complete surprise. Modern, muted pastel colours. A thick, soft carpet in cream. And beautiful photographs of wildlife adorning the walls. There was a small reception desk, three or four comfy chairs with a coffee table filled with magazines, a coffee machine, and a couple of closed doors. Maisie went behind the counter.

"What takes your fancy, Daphne? A full body massage? Hot stone treatment? There are a dozen or so options."

"Actually, I did have something in mind for Sunday morning, if you are open?"

"Always open. I live up here and don't mind working odd hours." Maisie was in her forties and had such a nice smile. It was impossible not to warm to her. "What were you thinking?"

"My husband is on the fishing trip until tomorrow afternoon and then we have the gala dinner to attend. But I wondered if I could book us both in for a massage before we leave on Sunday? If that isn't inconvenient?"

Maisie opened a book and ran her finger down a page. "Is nine too early? My assistant is here a bit before then so we can look after you both at the same time. We'll need forty-five minutes, and you will both feel so relaxed you'll want a nap."

"Sounds perfect. Although we'll need to head off soon after so don't relax John too much as he drives when we're towing Bluebell."

"Bluebell is a caravan?" Maisie hunted around the counter for something.

"She is. Our blue and white home away from home. Do you need a pen?"

"Pencil. Ah, there you are." Maisie reached down to the carpet. "What is your room number, Daphne?"

"Seventy-six."

"Such a nice suite! I love the views from it. And do you have any vouchers?"

Daphne had them in her hand. "There's one for each of us."

"You're here for the conference. And there's one spare. What about something for you?" Her finger returned to the page. "Not much today, I'm afraid—everyone wants a treatment, it seems. But there's a break in the conference timetable between twelve and two tomorrow. I could do a neck massage. Or a nice hand massage. Or refresh your make up?"

Now that she thought about it, her neck was a little stiff.

Maisie continued, "Tell me when you arrive. They all take the same length of time. So, what about one fifteen? Give you time to have lunch and I'll have you out of here half an hour later."

It was all so easy to do, this new, if temporary, life of being indulged. Treated like royalty. Between the beautiful suite, the welcome package, and not one but two day spa appointments, Daphne wanted to do a little dance. She left Maisie with a wave and continued her exploration.

The tennis courts were full, with people waiting nearby in small groups. Several teams played croquet. A lovely, natural looking swimming pool had a dozen or so guests floating on blow-up shapes or else lounging on sunbeds. Past all of this was a secluded garden in the style of those she'd seen on television in English shows about grand homes or else footage of the royal family. Manicured, green, and very formal.

Nobody else was around and Daphne settled on a stone bench beneath an expansive tree. High, perfectly trimmed hedges kept the sounds of the tennis court and pool at bay. A large, five-tiered fountain cascaded into a shallow pool surrounded by more red bricks. At its top was a peculiar looking statue of a man. He stood straight-backed, wearing a bowler hat and suit, with a briefcase in one hand, and he pointed, with the other, back toward the main building. From here it was impossible to see over the hedges to the exact place he indicated.

The strange contrasts added to the charm of the property.

Daphne's phone beeped and she unlocked it.

> We are at the river. They call the tents glamming tents. Very swish, will send a pic soon.

She messaged John.

> Sounds fancy! I'm sitting in a very English garden.

After taking a couple of photos she tapped send. There was only a couple of bars on her phone and the message didn't go. They'd been warned mobile coverage was sketchy. At least she knew John was safe and ready for his long-awaited fishing time.

She wandered back to the hotel, cutting across lawns broken up with flower beds. At the edge of the driveway, she stopped as an emptiness filled her stomach. Not hunger. It was a sense of being alone. Daphne didn't mind being on her own, but this was different.

You're too used to John being with you all the time.

This was true. Not only had they spent many years working in close proximity, but in recent months they'd spent no more than a couple of hours apart.

He'll be back tomorrow.

So why did that empty feeling sink lower? She glanced around, expecting to find someone watching her but everyone was going about their business. There was no reason for dread. Nothing was going to happen to John unless he fell into the river like Rupert Witherspoon had suggested. And John was too careful for that.

What she needed was a refreshing shower, a change of clothes, and a trip to the bar to meet up with the other attendees. No moping around or imagining the worst. This was her time, and nothing was going to stop her enjoying every minute.

FIVE

DINNER WITH A DIFFERENCE

"There she is!" Rupert's voice boomed across a room filled with people, laughter, and chatting. He rose from a barstool and waved at Daphne, who had paused in the doorway at the sight of so many strangers.

There was no going back now, so she planted a smile on her face and weaved past other tables and seats in his direction.

He stepped forward and kissed her cheek as if they were long-lost friends. "Don't you look lovely? Fresh as a daisy."

"Oh? Well, thank you." She'd taken twenty minutes to decide on her favourite wide-legged black pants with a white blouse patterned with pretty butterflies. And for once she'd chosen a higher heeled shoe. Confidence. All about confidence.

Rupert wore a red velvet jacket over a silk shirt with its top two buttons undone which exposed a few white chest hairs and a gold chain, and his hair was loose from its ponytail. Somehow, the look suited him.

"Daphne Jones, let me introduce you to some of the wonderful people behind the association. This is Audrey Sutton, Gloria Long, and Stacy Chester. What would you care to drink, Daphne? A glass of champagne?"

"Just some sweet white wine, thank you."

He pulled over a barstool from an empty table. "Sit, and get to know each other."

Rupert disappeared toward the bar and Daphne perched on the edge of the rather high barstool, gripping her handbag.

Three sets of eyes scrutinised her. Three mouths pursed up. And then glances were exchanged. This was disconcerting. Nobody spoke. Well, somebody had to.

"I'm so excited to be here. And I think I've heard all of your names before." She settled a bit more comfortably on the stool. "Audrey, am I right that you are the vice president?"

The woman she addressed nodded. Silver hair in a sleek chignon, she couldn't have been more than forty. Elegant drop earrings with multiple diamonds complemented a pendant. Daphne knew her gemstones and her estimation of the value of the set would have deterred her from ever wearing them without a bodyguard.

"And Gloria, you are the treasurer?"

"Yes, honey. I manage the funds." Gloria was around her own age. With rich brown hair in a classic bob, she had long fingers covered in rings and a thickset waist.

The third woman reached her hand over the table to shake. "I'm Stacy. I look after the members and was the person who had the privilege of seeing the glowing recommendation about you which resulted in the complimentary tickets and free accommodation. So nice to meet you!" Younger than any of them, Stacy spoke fast and was thin with shoulder-length, straight brown hair, and small round glasses. In a bright yellow blouse and blue skirt, she didn't wear makeup and barely made eye contact with Daphne, grabbing a glass and sipping as soon as the handshake finished.

"It is lovely to meet you. Are you all celebrants?"

"Only Gloria, and of course, Rupert," Audrey said. She played with the stem of a martini. "My husband is a celebrant and I enjoy being able to serve the association, but my thing is wedding gowns, which does fit well with all of this."

Rupert returned with a glass of wine which he set before

Daphne, and some red concoction with an umbrella for himself. "When Audrey says wedding gowns, she means Sutton Brides."

She recognised the name as being a chain of top end bridal shops. Suddenly, the diamonds made sense. Daphne had heard more than one bride wish they could afford a Sutton gown.

"Why don't you tell us about yourself?" Rupert settled on his barstool and curled both hands around his drink. "We know little about you prior to joining the association and since you did, you've made quite a splash."

Not sure if I want this on my bio.

"Um, well, I married my high school sweetheart, and we ran a business together for a long time. Rivers End Real Estate. John is well thought of in real estate circles. We retired and refurbished a caravan and now we travel so I can officiate. He fishes, and takes photographs, and loves genealogy."

"And do you have a family back in Rivers End?" Stacy asked, eyes still on her drink.

"Sadly, no children. We fostered for many years."

"Can't imagine putting up with someone else's kid," Audrey said. "Bad enough having one's own."

What a sad way to feel.

"How many children do you have, Audrey?" Daphne asked sweetly.

"Me? None, thank goodness. Happy to be an aunt but happier to keep it that way."

"You are missing out on so much, honey," Gloria said. "My five kids are the reason I get up every day."

"To make them breakfast and pack their lunches," Audrey countered.

"Well, they all have their own families now so no more packing lunches, but I do miss it. Daphne, you mentioned you fostered? I imagine that was rewarding?"

It was the best time in Daphne's life, apart from the recent move to the nomadic life. Bringing stability and gentle boundaries to the lives of displaced youngsters, seeing their confidence and self-respect grow… rewarding didn't begin to express it. Even when they moved on, it was almost always with a happiness for their new start. Almost always.

"Daphne?" Gloria spoke again.

"Oh, sorry! Yes. Rewarding on many levels."

Even when one of them leaves a hole in your heart.

She drank some wine. "Thank you, Rupert."

"Let's have a toast." Rupert raised his glass. "To new friends and delightful company!"

An hour later, all five were seated around a different table in the restaurant.

Rupert invited the women to join him for dinner and Daphne had to admit she had warmed up to him. And liked the women. Although Audrey was harder to get to know, as she was tapping away on her phone for most of the time. The reception was better in the bar and when Daphne visited the ladies, she sent a quick message to John to wish him a nice evening.

The restaurant was on the roof of the hotel, with plenty of floor to ceiling windows to capture the wonderful views in what was left of the long evening light. Most tables were full and there was much waving and called greetings between people who clearly knew each other. With an annual conference it made sense celebrants would become friends when attending, though she was being quiet. It was somewhat overwhelming.

Talk turned to the conference itself and immediately, Audrey excused herself. "Time to circulate."

Once she'd moved to another table, Stacy finally looked up with a small smile. "Much better."

"Aw, you mustn't let her bother you, Stace." Gloria patted Stacy's shoulder. "Everyone knows what she's like."

I don't. But I can guess.

Rupert said nothing. His eyes drifted to Audrey then to Daphne, smiling when she tilted her head in question. He filled a glass with wine for himself and topped up Daphne's without asking.

"Anyway, I'm looking forward to the first session," Stacy said. "Managing a wedding day crisis."

Gloria laughed. "Would have been handy when I did my very first wedding. Bride didn't even show up, leaving a confused groom and a garden filled with arguing relatives. Ah, the good old days."

"Daphne should have been the presenter." Stacy was a different person without Audrey around. Her eyes sparkled and she smiled. "You had a murder!"

"True. But I'd rather it had been a straightforward ceremony. I muddled through rather than anything else and am keen to take notes."

"You are too humble. I happen to know you have helped solve murders in two towns and put yourself in the path of danger both times. Which you shouldn't do, not really, but I do admire you!" Stacy said. "I wish I was nearly as brave."

Dinner arrived. Plates piled high with battered or grilled fish, depending on preference, hand cut potato wedges, and aioli for dipping.

"Freshly caught from the river," Rupert noted. "Which hopefully nobody has fallen into." He grinned at Daphne, and she smiled back at the small joke.

Audrey returned when she noticed her plate had arrived. Stacy dropped her eyes again and concentrated on her food. What on earth was going on between the two women? Stacy was either afraid of Audrey, or there'd been bad feelings between them. Not that Audrey gave any indicator she cared. If anything, there was the hint of a smile on her lips. Or was it a sneer?

Stop seeing things that aren't there.

"When does Darren arrive, Audrey?" Gloria asked.

Audrey glanced at her diamond encrusted watch. "Who knows? He had a wedding today which is a four-hour drive away. I might go and make sure one of the staff is waiting down at the carpark."

"I heard you arrange it earlier, Auds," Rupert said. "No point hassling them."

"Reminding. *Rupes*. Reminding. There's a distinct lack of respect toward me from certain members of the front desk staff and I won't have my husband left standing about in the dark on his own." She stood, picking up her glass of wine. "The food is ordinary. For now." With that she stalked away in stilettos which wobbled as she weaved around tables.

"Apologies, Daphne." Rupert sighed. "Audrey will be much happier once her husband arrives. She worries about him—"

"You mean she imagines he's off with someone else." Stacy spoke to her plate.

Rupert waved that away. "Regardless. We are all one big celebrant and partners family. Now, people. Dinner won't eat itself."

Well, well, well. There were cracks in the veneer of the executive. Rupert calling them all family rang alarm bells. In Daphne's experience, families were the worst when it came to secrets, grudges, and deception. Not that anything would or could go wrong here in this beautiful hotel.

Never.

SIX

MIDNIGHT MOVES

Dessert was so delicious Daphne wished she could send a plate of it to John. Three tiny offerings. A chocolate mousse. A crème brûlée. And the creamiest vanilla ice cream ever.

"All made in-house." Gloria mentioned as she scooped up some of her mousse. "It surely is one of the reasons we book here year after year."

"This and the view," Rupert added.

He had removed his jacket and rolled up his sleeves before dessert arrived. The restaurant was warm with so many guests and plenty of waiting staff hurrying to and from the kitchen. Daphne appreciated her choice of clothing and stayed hydrated with water in between glasses of wine. Of which she'd had three. Any more and she knew she'd get the giggles.

Audrey had returned from her trip downstairs to reception but joined another group and was laughing a lot. There were ongoing calls for toasts and clinking of glasses coming from that direction. Stacy had glanced over when Audrey first came back to the roof, but then she relaxed. Or it might be the five or six glasses of wine she'd consumed. Not one to judge, Daphne let the others talk, nodding if they looked her way. It was pleasant and friendly, and she was happy she'd come out to dinner tonight.

Guests began to leave and wait staff cleared the tables.

"Let's sit out on the roof." Rupert was already on his feet, jacket in one hand and glass in the other. "Pleasant weather tonight."

"I might say goodnight." This was Gloria. "Like Daphne, my husband is off fishing, and I have a paperback I'm keen to finish seeing as I have the room to myself."

Spending time with a book was tempting and there was a nice selection in the suite. But she was relaxed and comfortable with the little group and not ready to head back yet. Daphne stood.

"I've enjoyed your company, Gloria. I imagine our husbands are swapping fishing stories around a campfire."

"Ted loves a good yarn, so I think you are right."

With Stacy and Rupert, Daphne wandered from the restaurant. A handful of other guests were seated out here so they found a table and chairs at the furthest end and settled down. The air was still warm and the sky cloudy. It didn't feel like rain was coming but it was a pity not to stargaze from this elevated position.

"This is almost the best part of being a member." Stacy stretched her arms wide and high. "Good company. Mostly. And this place."

"How often have you been here?"

"This is the fifth conference here and I've attended each one."

"Did you say earlier you aren't a celebrant?"

"Not the best job for me. I'm too shy sometimes and don't have the way with words people like you and Rupert do."

Rupert patted Stacy's arm. "Sweet of you to say." He turned to Daphne. "Stacy is the only paid member of the association. Although all the executives have a small expense account, we are all volunteers. But Stacy is employed to manage the legal aspects of the association and anything which falls outside the scope of the volunteers. Most of us are busy and Stacy makes our lives easier."

"Which means I get to see the good, bad, and the ugly! I deal with compliments and complaints. I'm the person who members go to if they are having any issues either with their work or with another member… which rarely happens, thank goodness. And I get to read all the glowing testimonials from clients." Stacy picked up her empty wine glass and frowned at it. "And this year, many have come from your own. I might get another. Anyone else?"

"Um, no. I'm fine, thanks," Daphne said.

Stacy disappeared into the restaurant.

"Are you less worried about John?" Rupert asked.

"John is a capable man."

"And you have a big heart."

This was true. Daphne loved people and loved giving and making others happy. She wasn't a proud woman, but she was realistic and knew herself pretty well at her age.

A burst of loud laughter had both of them turning to look at a table closer to the restaurant. Audrey was on her feet, somewhat unsteady, glass raised. "To people who can't find their way up a mountain. To Darren!"

"Oh dear. So, he hasn't arrived," Rupert said. "She might laugh about it, but Audrey will be fuming. I should consider having a cigar on my balcony to make myself scarce before she asks me to gather a search party."

Rupert was an interesting man. His voice was cultured—for want of a better term. Private education. Old money. Over dinner he'd mentioned a career in law and his early retirement to pursue his passion for art and officiating. There was no Mrs Witherspoon, and no children. He had three cats and lived on a houseboat. He also cared about those in the association he presided over.

"Stacy is nice," Daphne said.

"She is. But she sometimes allows other people's opinions to weigh on her."

About to ask if he meant Audrey's opinions, the reappearance of Stacy reminded Daphne she wasn't here to snoop into other people's lives. It wasn't as though there was a crime to solve.

"Well, that was a waste of the walk because the bar is closed, so I'm going to my room. You are both welcome to join me to raid the mini bar." Stacy reached for her handbag.

"Thank you for the offer, but I hear my bed calling, dear." Daphne pushed herself to her feet. "Never slept in a four-poster bed so I want to make the most of it."

Rupert stood. "Goodnight then. I shall finish my drink. Watch out for the moon for a while in case it makes an appearance. I shall see you ladies tomorrow."

When Stacy and Daphne reached the elevator, she turned. Rupert leaned against the brickwork surrounding the seated area, staring off into the night.

They stepped out of the elevator on the accommodation floor and Stacy went straight to the window overlooking the front of the hotel. It was a pleasant spot here with armchairs and coffee tables.

"Such a nice evening, even with the clouds. We should get a bottle of wine and find somewhere to drink it under a tree."

"Outside?"

"Like a nighttime picnic. But with wine. Or champagne. Except I drank mine yesterday." She turned with a wide smile. "Did you get a bottle as part of your welcome package?"

Yes. And it is staying in the fridge to share with John.

"Which is your room, Stacy? Would you like me to walk there with you?"

"Oh, you don't need to mother me. I'm just happy. I guess I'll see you in the morning."

"If you're sure."

"I am. Goodnight, Daphne. It's been a lot of fun."

Not entirely convinced, Daphne nevertheless needed to use her bathroom and figured Stacy was safe enough to find her way to her room. At the far corner she glanced back and Stacy waved.

Her suite was a welcome sight, and she kicked off her shoes with a sigh.

She popped on the kettle then hurried to the bathroom. A few minutes later she returned, makeup off and ready for a cuppa. A quick check of her phone was a little disappointing. Nothing from John. And only one bar of reception.

"Sleep tight, love." She blew a kiss into the air.

She opened the French doors and took a look out at the night but the sound of a door closing nearby reminded her that Rupert intended to have a cigar and she wasn't inclined to let the smoke drift into the suite. She closed the doors again.

While the tea brewed, she ran a finger over the selection of books, pulling out a few to read their back cover.

"A missing man. No body. No clues. And a daughter determined to find the truth. *Last Known Contact*. Oh, you sound promising." She tucked the book under her arm and carried her cup to one of the seats near the window. "Nothing like a mystery to solve while I drink my tea."

How pleasant this was. A beautiful suite with soft, thick carpet to curl her toes into. A nice cup of tea. And a new book.

Deeply engrossed in the fifth chapter, she jumped at a sound from the hallway. Reading a suspense late at night was enough to make anyone a little jumpy. But it was as though someone had stopped outside her door. Leaned on it, or turned the handle.

"John?"

Daphne scrambled to her feet. Had something happened and he was back? He hadn't taken the extra key.

"Is that you, John?"

No answer. And all was quiet. She opened the door and peered down the hallway. Nobody and nothing. Just her imagination.

After closing the door, she stepped on something flat and pliable.

"Oh, my. Where did you come from?"

She scooped up an envelope and carried it back to her chair, where the light was better. It hadn't been there when she came in.

Well, she was pretty sure it wasn't. A note from reception? Or someone from the conference?

The envelope was plain and sealed so she opened it and drew out a folded piece of paper. There was writing on one side. Actually, there was a map on half of the paper and writing above it.

"Grab your shoes and find me. S.C.," she read aloud. "Stacy?"

There was a poem.

> Come to the fountain
> at the top of the mountain
> We will dance and sing
> Until morning we bring
> Meet me now if you dare
> For sweet moments to share

"What on earth?" Little made sense. "Until morning we bring? Not very good poetry. Or the ramblings of someone who drank too much!"

If it was Stacy, then she'd better go and check the woman was all right because she'd had a fair bit to drink and might fall into the fountain if she was galivanting around it inebriated.

The map was a rough overlay of the grounds of the hotel. The tennis court and day spa were marked with an X. As was the English garden where she'd sat this afternoon to enjoy the quiet. Yesterday afternoon. It was after midnight.

She peered through the window and sure enough, there was Stacy heading into the darkness toward the tennis court.

Daphne went in search of sensible shoes.

SEVEN

THE FOUNTAIN ATOP A MOUNTAIN

Daphne collected her phone, the note, and the key for the door. Nothing worse than finding herself locked out on her return. She went out onto the balcony in the hope of seeing Rupert, but his French doors were closed and no lights shone through.

Despite this, she tapped on his suite door a moment later. Perhaps he'd help her find Stacy, but all was silent and when she leaned her ear against the door, there was not even the sound of snoring. Assuming he snored, of course.

She walked down the stairs rather than wait for what she'd discovered was a slow elevator. The office behind the reception desk was closed and although the sign she'd seen earlier about opening again at six had an emergency phone number, she was hardly going to wake someone over this.

Outside, she followed the driveway until the path to the garden veered off. She crunched her way over the small pebbles, passing the day spa and then stopping near the dark, deserted tennis courts.

This was one of the spots marked on the map with an X.

She opened the flashlight app on her phone and flicked the light around. No movement or sign of anything out of the ordinary.

Whatever that might be.

The poem said nothing about tennis courts, though.

A shiver ran up her spine and she turned off the flashlight and gazed around. Surely nobody was watching her?

"Stacy?"

Silence. What if there was someone else out here? Out here in the dark in the middle of the night.

Alone in the dark in a strange place. Good one, Daph.

She was here now. Daphne turned the flashlight back on.

"Find Stacy and go to bed," she muttered and started walking again, before she could change her mind.

Ahead, the high, perfectly manicured hedges were like a wall. There was an archway leading in and beneath it, Daphne hesitated, peering into the gloom.

"Stacy? It's Daphne Jones."

Her flashlight moved around her in a semi-circle as she looked for signs of Stacy. As she turned, her peripheral vision picked up the shape of a person looming in the dark and she squealed and almost dropped her phone.

Get a grip, Daph. It's a statue!

Statue or not, between that and the low, scudding clouds, this garden was getting creepier by the minute. Putting a hand over her heart, which thudded painfully, she took a couple of long breaths through her nose. Her friend Charlotte was a psychiatrist and once told her gulping air through her mouth after a scare might make her feel worse as it sparks off a person's fight or flight instinct. Good advice.

As her fright subsided, she considered her options. The most appealing one was to retrace her steps and hightail it back to the comfort and safety of her suite. But what if Stacy was no longer in a condition to get back on her own?

Best to check the fountain. It would only take a minute.

All was quiet.

"Well, that is odd."

The fountain wasn't splashing. No water flowed.

Moonlight suddenly streamed through a break in the clouds.

A person sat on the bricks surrounding the base of the fountain. A woman, staring into the water.

"Stacy? What's wrong, dear?"

Stacy raised an arm and pointed into the fountain without looking at Daphne, who hurried to join her. She peered into the water and her heart stopped.

Oh no. Oh no!

There was a red jacket floating on the surface.

Was it covering a body?

A body in the water?

"Rupert!"

The clouds closed up again, plunging the garden back into murky darkness.

"Stacy! Stacy, look at me!"

Stacy did more than that. She jumped to her feet and grabbed Daphne's hands with wet, icy cold fingers. Her glasses were missing and her eyes, as she leaned close, were wide and alarmed.

"Need... need help. Please. Get help."

"Are you alright, Stacy? Are you hurt?"

"I'm okay. But it's too late for..." She gulped. "Please get someone."

Releasing Daphne's hands, Stacy turned back to the fountain.

There were no bars on Daphne's phone.

"I'll be right back."

She turned and ran back through the archway.

Someone called her name, and she glanced back. Nobody. Just an over-active imagination.

Her feet flew along the pebbled path.

Past the tennis courts.

In sight of the hotel, she had to slow down as a stitch clutched at her side.

Keep going.

The sweet yet irritating smell of cigar smoke reached her nostrils, and her eyes shot up to Rupert's balcony.

It was in darkness, as was the suite. But smoke drifted away from the building and there was the slightest movement as a chair scraped on tiles.

"Daphne? Is that you down there?"

Mouth open, she stopped dead, sucking in air.

"Whatever are you doing out there so late?" he asked.

Rupert leaned over the balcony.

Relief poured into her. "You're not dead!"

A pause and then a chuckle. "I sincerely hope not, buttercup. Did you join Stacy at her mini bar?"

Everything began to spin and she had to brace her legs as the world tilted. What was going on? If it wasn't Rupert in the fountain, then who?

"I'm coming down, Daphne. Find a spot to sit and I'll be there in a minute."

Sit? There wasn't time to sit. Some poor soul had died and she had to get help.

She focused on her breathing. Long, slow, deep breaths. She took her glasses off and blinked a few times, then slid them on again. The ground was steady. She wasn't going to fall. This was all a terrible shock, but she had to pull herself together and find a way to make sense of this.

Except... who was in the fountain?

If only John was here.

"Daphne? Tell me what's wrong." Rupert—wrapped up in the same dressing gown as earlier in the day—hurried from the hotel.

"I... there is so much to tell you. But I'm not drunk. The fountain. I was in my suite. And the note. And I found her there. And the body."

Rupert put his hands on her shoulders and leaned down to make her look at his eyes. "What body?"

Her mouth opened and shut again, and she grabbed one of his

hands from her shoulder. "Come and see." She tugged at him when he hesitated. "Stacy."

"Stacy? Oh my—"

"Not her. I don't know who. But she's there. In shock."

Despite his attire, and a pair of slippers on his feet, Rupert wasted no more time and Daphne had to jog to keep up with him. They made it back to the English garden and to the fountain even faster than she'd managed in reverse moments ago.

"Where's Stacy?" Rupert removed his slippers. "Do you have any light?"

Between gasps for oxygen—this running back and forth was exhausting—Daphne turned her phone's flashlight on and waved it around. No sign of anyone.

"Can you shine it in here, please?" Rupert stepped into the fountain.

"Should you do that? This might be a crime scene."

Daphne turned the light onto the red velvet coat as Rupert leaned down. Water lapped up his calves, the dressing gown just out of danger of dipping in. It was the strangest thing. The coat had floated further around the fountain but where was the body?

Rupert grunted as he dragged the jacket out. "Ruined." Water poured from it as he stepped out and laid it on the grass.

"I don't understand." She walked right around the fountain, flashlight on the water. "Where is the body?"

"Which body, Daphne? And where is Stacy?"

An excellent question.

"The top of the bricks are wet here." She was on the opposite side to Rupert, and he joined her, slippers in one hand as he tried to dry his other hand on the dressing gown. "All along this side."

Rupert put his slippers on, grimacing as they stuck to his damp feet. "I would appreciate an explanation for all of this. My jacket in the fountain. You running around like you've seen a ghost. And what does Stacy have to do with this?"

Her mind raced. Stacy was here earlier. They'd spoken. Had

physical contact. And there'd been a body... or had there? The jacket. Yes. But had she actually seen a person under the surface?

"Daphne! Oh, Rupert. Rupert, you're alive!"

Stacy sort-of sprinted from the opposite direction. She was unsteady on her feet and her arms waved around.

"Of course, I'm alive," Rupert muttered then he grabbed Stacy as she threw herself at him. Well, fell in his direction. He helped her stand upright. "Why do both of you believe I am deceased? Come on, ladies, it's enough to make a man feel he's more than just slightly over the hill!"

"It was your jacket in the fountain. I saw it and thought it was you in there," Daphne said. "But Stacy, where is the body? Was there really a body in there?"

"Didn't you hear me calling? I hadn't wanted to leave." Stacy pointed in the direction she'd run from. "They must have carried him through there. I came after you to ask you to look out for my glasses. I lost them somewhere. But I got as far as the tennis courts and couldn't see you and came back to find... to find nothing."

Rupert glanced at Daphne with a frown. Worry, perhaps. "How about we go back to the hotel and get you warmed up, Stace? Your hands are freezing."

"Yes, and I can make you some tea," Daphne said.

"But we need to find whoever was in the fountain. Can we call the police?"

"Not from here, dear. No signal."

"Then you both need to come with me and help look. I'm sure whoever took the body went through the gap in the corner."

"Who is dead and why would anyone take their body?" Rupert asked.

Oh no, not this again! Not after last time.

Only recently, Daphne had attended a funeral where the deceased failed to arrive for their own burial. This wasn't the same, though. There had been someone in the water. Hadn't there? With each passing moment she second-guessed herself a bit more. She'd seen the jacket with both arms moving in the water. Stacy had said there was a body. But had she seen one? A foot, or hand? Hair?

"Stacy. Did you slide a note under my door earlier?" she asked, reaching into her pocket where she'd shoved it earlier.

"Of course not. I don't even know which room you have."

"It's just that someone left a map pointing here with a poem and signed S.C. I thought you were out here all alone and after you'd had so much to..." She bit her lip.

"You think I am drunk?" Stacy threw her arms in the air. "What? That I imagined all of this? Well, fine then." She stormed off—not very convincingly—into the darkness in the wrong direction before doing a U-turn and stalking past Daphne and Rupert, again apparently lost. "We won't bother looking for murderers and body thieves."

"Shall we help her find the way back?" Rupert asked. "Won't be the first time she's had adventures after a few wines."

Much as she wanted more information about that, Daphne nodded, and they set out after Stacy.

EIGHT
NOBODY. NO BODY

With all her heart, Daphne wished John were here with her. She'd checked her phone for coverage several times but there wasn't enough to make a call, although she did try to send a message. It failed to go but probably would eventually.

She sat in the lobby of the hotel with Stacy and Rupert. All had cups of tea thanks to Maisie, who'd been the staff member rostered on for emergencies. Rupert hadn't hesitated to step behind the reception desk and use the landline to call for help. Maisie had told them to stay put and then she'd woken other staff.

By now it was after one in the morning and exhaustion had chased off any remaining adrenaline. Stacy nodded off in an armchair, covered by a blanket Maisie had found, and Mandy appeared, followed by Col.

After going over the events of the past hour or so with them, Daphne still had no idea what she'd seen earlier. Col went to wake another of the staff to go on a search around the fountain. Mandy was quiet until after he'd left and Maisie had gone to get more tea. Then, she moved to a seat closer to Daphne and Rupert.

"We need to get Stacy back to her room. No point upsetting her if anyone else comes down and starts asking questions." Mandy glanced at Rupert. "I doubt Col will find anything. This is just like last year. Do you remember?"

He nodded. "She was convinced somebody had stolen the association's laptop she had left in the conference room. Got it in her head it was somewhere outside at night and eventually we found her wandering along a bush track."

Mandy got to her feet. "I'll get a key to her room and be back, if you don't mind helping me wake her."

Once she was gone, Rupert leaned toward Daphne. "How did you know where she was?"

"I saw her leave the hotel. But before then, I heard someone at my door and found the note slid under it. When I saw the initials, I thought it must be her. She'd suggested when we left the roof that we take a bottle of champagne out and have a picnic."

He rolled his eyes. "I think our Stacy has had too much to drink tonight. You didn't actually see a body?"

Had she?

"I saw your jacket. The arms were floating as if your... I mean, a body, was in them. How did it get into the fountain, I wonder?"

"I left it on the roof. Didn't even remember until I dragged it out of the water. Ah, here's Col." Rupert stood and offered his hand to Daphne and she took it gratefully to let him help her up. All that running left both her knees aching and there was a definite crunch from one of them.

Col and another man came through the hotel door, locking it behind themselves. Col gave his flashlight to his co-worker, who walked past everyone with a shake of his head as though expressing he was unimpressed to be dragged from his bed.

"Nothing. Went up through the corner of the garden but there's no sign anyone was around. Found this." Col raised a hand holding an unopened champagne bottle. "Think our friend there forgot it." He put the bottle on a side table. "Want a hand getting her back to her room? Again?"

"Is that you, Col Colly Colin?" Stacy raised her head. "And Rupie. Are we going to open the bottle?"

"Not tonight. How about Col and I get you back to the comfort of your room? You can settle down for a proper sleep."

"Sure. I am tired." She pushed aside the blanket and yawned. "My glasses are missing. I might go for a quick walk and find them."

Mandy was back. "We'll track them down in daylight. Come on, then. Time for bed. I'll help Rupert."

"I have my keys." Col rattled a large metal ring of keys clipped to his belt but when Mandy didn't answer he shrugged and headed in the direction the other man had gone.

Stacy sang to herself as Mandy helped her to her feet and Rupert took her arm. He gave Daphne a half-smile as they slowly made their way to the elevator and mouthed, 'Breakfast?' She nodded back even though at this point she had no idea what would happen in the morning.

Maisie appeared with tea and looked around. "Oh. Well, would you like some more?"

Daphne blinked a few times. What she wanted was to have a cry. Not from emotion but tiredness. But she didn't want to offend the other woman, who'd been so helpful and acted as though looking after errant guests in the small hours was normal.

"You know, I think you might enjoy a sleep more than more caffeine. Would you like me to walk up with you?" Maisie put the tray down with a smile. "What a difficult evening you've had. I can assure you it isn't normally like this here. And I'm quite sure there is no mysterious body to be found. Poor Stacy just had a bit of a shock."

Haven't we all?

"May I have a raincheck on the tea? I really would like to climb into bed."

"Well, seeing as we have a beauty appointment tomorrow, I shall make sure to arrange the nicest tea leaves, and a few little treats to enjoy when you arrive." Maisie led the way to the elevator and pressed the up button. "You try and get a few hours' sleep before the conference begins."

The conference was last on her list of things to worry about. Daphne forced a smile. "Thank you for being so helpful. I'll see you tomorrow. Today. Later." The doors opened and she stepped inside.

An annoying, incessant tapping noise woke Daphne. She pulled the sheet over her head. How soft were these sheets? Eyes tightly shut, sleep called again. Just another few minutes and then she'd get up.

"Daphne... wake up call."

Pushing the sheet aside, Daphne sat up and opened her eyes, squinting at the light.

"I'll leave my door open." It was Rupert, outside her front door. "Come and join Gloria and me for breakfast in twenty minutes. We all need to talk."

"Okie dokie. Be there in twenty." She managed to call out although her throat was dry. Twenty minutes to shower, dry her hair, do make up and throw on clothes? No time for her morning coffee. A glass of water would have to do.

Out of bed, she stretched and winced as the creaky knee complained. Her ankles ached and her neck was sore. Thank goodness for the appointment later with Maisie. Definitely a neck massage. She couldn't resist a quick look from the balcony. A couple of people were out running and one of the hotel's 4WD's nosed past them in the direction of the gate. Cherry was driving. More guests must be on their way. It was a nice morning with blue skies.

It was more than twenty minutes later when she tapped on Rupert's open door, running her other hand through curls which refused to sit right. She'd foregone the makeup and straightening and was thankful it was only a bit after seven so she still had time to finish getting ready.

"There you are, Daphne. Go through to the living room." Rupert didn't look as though he'd only had a few hours' sleep. He wore a linen shirt and pants, and his hair was in a small bun at his nape.

Gloria was seated at a small dining table and she waved as Daphne approached. "Morning, honey. Come and sit down and Rupert can make you a coffee."

"What would you like?" Rupert had closed the front door and was now at a coffee machine. He had a proper—if tiny—kitchen. "Black. Cappuccino. Latte?"

"Oh, a latte would be wonderful, thank you." Daphne joined Gloria at the table which was filled with enticing bowls of sliced fruit, yoghurt, and a plate of pastries.

Gloria reached for the fruit and began spooning some into a smaller bowl. "There's eggs, bacon, toast and the like under the cloches on the trolley, so help yourself to whatever you fancy." She nodded at a waiter's trolley to one side. "I keep saying the food here is one of the best reasons to visit."

"As well as the suite. The bed was rather nice."

"I imagine after such an adventure last night that any bed would have felt good."

Adventure was one word for it. Once Daphne had reached her suite, she'd virtually fallen into bed. Even her clothes ended up on the floor, something she would never normally do.

"One latte." Rupert placed a glass mug near Daphne. "Please eat. I ordered some of everything so there is plenty of food. I guessed you might have an appetite after all that running around during the night."

"Thank you. And yes. I am starving."

All of them attended to filling plates or bowls and ate for a few minutes in silence. Gloria was right about the food being delicious. Perfectly scrambled eggs, golden toast, and yummy fried tomatoes. And a pancake. Daphne had to stop herself after one in case she didn't fit into the dress she'd chosen for today.

Rupert dabbed his lips with a napkin then folded it and put it on his empty plate. "Nice way to start our busy day. This is a bit of a tradition, having breakfast in one of our suites—by that I mean mine, Gloria's, Audrey's, or Stacy's. With the situation overnight, I need to talk about Stacy without her here."

"And Audrey would enjoy this more than she should," Gloria added.

"I've updated Gloria on my recollection of events. Would you fill us both in on what happened from your perspective? I'll make us all another coffee first. Shall we sit on the balcony?"

A few minutes later, each with a coffee, they settled on Rupert's balcony which was twice the size of Daphne's and had access from the living area and the bedroom. A small group of hotel staff, including Col, were walking in the direction of the English garden.

"What if there was a body?" Daphne said, before she could filter the question.

"Did you see one?"

"I saw your jacket. That is crystal clear. The way it was in the water... it appeared to be covering something, and Stacy was adamant it was a body. But it was dark and when I went to take a closer look she jumped up and was agitated. Wanted me to get help." Try as she might, Daphne couldn't visualise a body in the water. Just the jacket. "So, I came back here with the intention of knocking on doors for someone to help me if I couldn't raise anyone by phone."

"Except you saw me."

"I could smell you."

Daphne bit her lip. How rude she was.

But Rupert threw back his head and laughed.

"Cigars again?" Gloria shook her head. "Just as well the hotel staff like you so much, breaking the rules at whim and bringing people here who have created havoc more than once."

He stopped laughing. "We aren't responsible for the actions of other adults."

Gloria raised one eyebrow and sipped her coffee.

"You don't just mean Stacy, do you?" he asked. Without waiting for an answer, he turned to Daphne. "We only met yesterday but it is clear how intuitive you are. I imagine you won't be surprised to hear Audrey has made life uncomfortable for Stacy in her role with the association."

"I gathered there is some ill feeling between them."

Tread lightly, Daph.

Gloria and Rupert exchanged a glance, and he nodded. "Last year, the night of the gala dinner—but after it officially ended—Audrey got worked up when Darren disappeared without a word. He was helping Stacy look for the laptop she'd thought was missing from the conference room. Turned out Audrey had picked it up for safekeeping, but nobody knew that."

"Why would she be upset about her husband helping look for association property?"

"She didn't care about the laptop. Audrey is rather possessive of Darren. He's considerably her senior and has been married several times. She tends to imagine the worst," Gloria said. "Anyway, she had words with both Darren and Stacy, rather publicly, and since then Stacy goes quiet when Audrey is around."

"I imagine they come into contact, though. With both having roles in the association?" Daphne asked.

"We only meet once a month—so not often. The role of the vice president is hardly onerous and she's not always present. I've yet to miss a meeting and am hands on, so Audrey doesn't have a lot to do with the day-to-day management of the association."

A position of power without much power. Daphne had come across people who took on a role on a committee or in a group more for the prestige of the title.

"That gives you insight into the awkwardness last night. When the two women are together, they are civil and represent the association appropriately," Gloria said. "Until Stacy decides she needs to wander around in the dead of night."

"Dead being the question." Rupert pointed in the direction Col and the others had taken.

"Has the hotel contacted the police?" Just in case.

Rupert nodded. "Yes. The closest station is about twenty kilometres away. Two towns from here."

"They might want to take their own look around and speak with Stacy and me. Not that I have much to offer."

"If there's nothing out of the ordinary uncovered in daylight and you can't confirm sighting a corpse in the fountain, then we have to put it down to Stacy having too much to drink. But we'll need to address this with her."

There was an ominous tone in Rupert's words. He glanced at his watch.

"I'm going to head down and do some last-minute preparations so will see you for the first session, Daphne."

Gloria held up her half-full cup. "I shall sit here and finish this. I'll lock the door."

Daphne stood. "And I must make myself presentable. Thank you for a lovely breakfast and company."

And a mystery. Maybe more than one.

NINE
AN ANGRY WOMAN

In the slow elevator on the way downstairs, a flutter of nerves surprised Daphne.

But I look nice. Hair and makeup done. And doesn't my dress fit well?

The latter was thanks to a few weeks of watching her food choices and walking a bit faster and further every day and it was worth it all to slip into her red polka dot dress and zip it up without too much holding her breath.

Although she'd been made to feel welcome by those she'd so far met, this was all new. Fifty or so people she hadn't met, most of them celebrants and no doubt far more experienced than she was. What if the speakers asked the audience questions and chose her?

Smile and nod a lot.

John always said she was a natural people person.

"Time to prove him right, Daphne Jones," she whispered as the doors opened in the foyer.

The first thing she saw was a large sign with an arrow pointing further into the hotel than she'd been. "Welcome to Celebrating Celebrants." There was a cute picture of a bride and groom on the sign.

She followed the arrow down a wide hallway to where a table

was set up with a woman sitting behind it, beside open double doors. The woman smiled as Daphne approached.

"Good morning and welcome! I'm Nancy. Now, I'm afraid I'm not very good at this but let's find you on the list and get you a lanyard." Nancy pushed a box filled with named lanyards closer. "Stacy normally handles the check-ins but hasn't appeared, so can you have a look for yours and I'll tick you off? What was your name?"

"Daphne Jones." She found her lanyard and put it over her head.

"Oh. You're her." Nancy stared.

Not certain she liked the sound of this, Daphne plastered on a wide smile. "I'm who?"

"You know." Nancy looked both ways, leaned forward, and whispered, "The sleuth."

Oh dear.

"Not really. I'm a celebrant. Retired from a real estate business. Past foster mother. Proud wife of a wonderful man. But hardly a sleuth."

"Not what I hear. No, I hear you solve crimes and help the police." Nancy returned to finding Daphne's name. "Ah, there you are." She put a tick against it. "Are you going to find any criminals here?"

The image of Rupert's jacket floating in the fountain flashed through her mind.

"I am quite certain this beautiful hotel has no criminals at all. In fact, I can't wait to listen to all the speakers and learn more about being a celebrant. So nice to meet you, Nancy."

"You, too. But I think there is something going on. After all, there were cars driving about and people wandering around right up until the wee hours of this morning. That isn't how innocent people act."

A small group approached along the hallway and Daphne smiled and stepped through the doorway, relieved for the excuse to leave Nancy to her musings. Hopefully, nobody else knew anything about her. What she'd said was true. She was here to learn.

"Ah, there's my buttercup."

I'm really not your buttercup.

Rupert waved from the front of the room, which was large with chandeliers, and windows covered with heavy curtains. He was adjusting a microphone at a podium on a low stage. There were rows of seats separated by an aisle leading to him and Daphne followed it. Only a couple of other people were in the room and they sat in the back row, talking.

"Hello again. Nancy said she hasn't seen Stacy yet. Is she alright?"

"Had a quick chat with her after our breakfast. There. Think that will stay still." He finished with the microphone. "She is adamant there is a body. Upset even that there isn't a police presence here. I told her someone has told the police and suggested she get a bit more sleep and come down during the morning tea break."

"And there isn't? Signs of... you know."

He shook his head. "Col and his team did a thorough search in and around the garden and nothing. Thank goodness."

"Yes."

Rupert folded his arms and smiled. "You look nice. Polka dots are in. Are you looking forward to the conference?"

"I am. But I'm also a bit... well, I feel I'm such a newbie."

He laughed. "Not one thing to worry about, Mrs Jones. Between you and me, most of the attendees are here for the food and the conversation. A lot only see each other at the conferences so there is catching up to be done and gossip to share. Most of them are friendly but don't be concerned if they are too busy with each other to get to know you."

"I have cookies."

Rupert's eyes lit up. "Where are you hiding them?"

"Upstairs. I made a couple of batches to bring as an ice breaker. Unless you think it is silly."

"Nothing silly about cookies. We have a break between both

morning sessions and there is a table being set up in the foyer with some nibbles, so why not add them to the offerings?"

There was nothing she wanted more. Well, apart from seeing John and working out exactly what happened last night. But cookies to share was a good start.

Daphne found a seat on the outside end of a middle row as the room filled. It wasn't long before Rupert made a short welcome speech and introduced the first speaker. She took out her notebook and pen. This was what she'd looked forward to and she wasn't going to miss a word.

The minute the clapping stopped, Daphne slipped out of the room and hurried to her suite. She collected the top container of cookies and was about to leave with them when her phone beeped. A message from John. She wanted to read it then and there but if she didn't get these onto the table it would be too late.

Back downstairs she found a spot on the table between scones and muffins and opened the lid. People were milling about in the hallway, getting coffee or tea, so she moved further along where it was quieter and checked the message.

> Only just got this, doll. Are you okay or would you like me to come back?

"Goodness, no."
She tapped out a reply.

> It was all a false alarm and everything is going well here. Just attended the first session. How is the fishing?

The response was quick. At least the reception was improved from last night.

> Pleased to hear all is well. Fishing is brilliant. Good company and food. Have you made some new friends?

Not certain she could yet classify anyone as a friend. She glanced at the table as she considered her response. People were helping themselves to the cookies. That was nice.

> Had a lovely breakfast with the president and the treasurer. Neck massage at lunch time. People are helping themselves to my cookies as we speak!

She fancied one herself with a cup of coffee. Although she'd had two lattes at breakfast, she was still tired and needed a caffeine kick. John sent back a love heart emoji and she replied with one of her own.

There was just time to pour a coffee before Rupert called everyone back in. Others were carrying their cups and nibbles and there were no cookies left. Not sure whether to be disappointed or elated, she chose the latter. If people loved her cookies, then she'd done a good job.

Partway through this session, she saw Stacy sneak in. She stood at the back of the room, looking around as if searching for someone. Heads turned and she quickly found a seat. It was good she was up and about and hopefully less upset than when Daphne last saw her.

The speaker was entertaining as she showed slides of some of the more elaborate weddings she'd officiated, including a cliff top affair as a thunderstorm rolled in. The photographs were stunning, but Daphne would have struggled to stay out in the open if there was lightning. Not a fan of storms when she was safely inside, let alone out at the mercy of the elements.

All too soon, Rupert was asking for a round of applause and announcing the lunch break. The room cleared faster than it had for morning tea and when Daphne followed, she understood why. Where morning tea had been served, a larger table was now in place with a buffet lunch and there was already a long line which she joined. She checked the time. Her appointment with Maisie was for one fifteen which was just under forty-five minutes away.

"Daphne. Daphne, I'm so glad you are still here."

Stacy was right behind her, her voice low and anxious, and Daphne turned to look at her. Up close, the other woman's eyes were red-rimmed behind her glasses and she wore no makeup.

"You found your glasses, dear."

"Oh. Oh, yes, they were in my room. But I don't remember leaving them there."

Her face was so worried that Daphne wanted to hug her, but perhaps here wasn't the place.

"Everyone is telling me I am mistaken about last night, but you were there. You saw."

A jacket in the water.

"Let's get some lunch and we can chat away from everyone."

"You don't want to be seen here with me? With the mad woman?" Stacy's voice rose and people turned around. A couple of them whispered to each other which agitated Stacy further. "Yes, a mad woman who imagines dead bodies that mysteriously disappear."

More whispers.

Daphne took Stacy's arm. "Why don't we go for a walk? Let's check the fountain ourselves."

"What's the point when nobody believes me?" Stacy stiffened. "Great. Just what I need."

Audrey headed their way, her eyes on Stacy and the glimmer of a smile on her lips. A rather unkind smile, in Daphne's opinion. This wasn't going to be pleasant.

"Then let's go for that walk." Daphne lowered her voice. "Don't allow her to distress you because I am not going to stand for any nonsense. You've done nothing wrong, so lift your chin and come with me. Please."

Gratitude brightened Stacy's face and she did just that, raising her head and smiling at Daphne as though they were having a lovely—and normal—conversation.

"Well, well. If it isn't our little panic merchant."

Audrey planted herself between them and freedom. Short of

pushing through the line, there was little to do but wait for the vice president to move.

"Good morning. Did your husband arrive safely?"

Audrey's face hardened. "I was going to ask Stacy if she'd seen him."

"Huh? Why would I?"

"Oh, I don't know. Middle of the night. Sneaking around outside. Claiming some crime has been committed. My husband nowhere to be seen. Ring any bells, Stacy?"

Stacy's head dropped, her eyes on the ground.

All around them, other guests were watching. Nobody was at the buffet as people inched closer to listen in.

"Audrey, I'm not sure here is the place to—" Daphne began.

"Excuse me? You've been a celebrant for two minutes and know nothing about the historical, and hysterical, behaviour of this woman! A woman we pay to manage our membership."

Audrey was wearing the same earrings as last night and the angrier she got, the more they swung from side to side. There was a stone missing from one. Surely it was there during dinner? Yes, the more Daphne looked at it, the more she was convinced the diamond had disappeared overnight. Like the body.

She forced down the urge to giggle. Angry people did that to her.

"Are you even listening to me, Daphne?" Audrey demanded, folding her arms.

Everyone is listening to you.

The earring stopped jingling about. Daphne straightened her back. "Stacy and I are going for a walk outside. Would you let us pass, please?" Keeping one's tone calm and rational usually took the wind from the sails of an unreasonable person. At least, that was her experience with the occasional difficult customer they'd had at work. Her aim was always to defuse rather than defend.

"Listen. I came over here to speak with Stacy, so you go and toddle off and eat one of your awful cookies on your walk. But Stacy stays."

Awful cookies? A chill settled in Daphne's stomach.

Stacy reached for her arm. Her head was still down and her anxiety showed in the tight grip she had on Daphne. Time for this silliness to stop. She smiled at the people closest to her in the line.

"May we squeeze past?"

There was an immediate gap made.

"Thank you so much. I do hope you enjoy the lunch. It looks delicious."

Expecting the vice president to object or follow, Daphne, with Stacy attached, hurried past the table and into the foyer. She glanced behind where Audrey still stood, arms crossed, glaring in their direction.

TEN

WHEN COOKIES AREN'T ENOUGH

"I can't do this anymore."

They were almost across the foyer when Stacy released Daphne's arm and stopped, raising her head to gaze around as though surprised at where they were.

Back in the hallway, Audrey was in conversation with Rupert, waving her arms around and sending death glares at Daphne and Stacy.

"I need to go back to my room. I need to pack."

They headed for the stairs and reached the accommodation floor without speaking. Audrey's behaviour was both strange and appalling. Leaving Stacy on her own didn't feel right.

"Let's go to my suite, Stacy. I'll make us some tea and I have some cookies to share. Or you can simply sit on the balcony alone if you don't want me fussing over you. Give you a chance to work out if you really wish to go."

Stacy followed without a word and when they reached her suite, she saw there were tears streaking her face.

"Oh, you poor dear, let's get you inside."

That accomplished, Stacy asked to use the bathroom. By the time she emerged, face washed but her eyes still bright, Daphne had put cookies onto a plate from the little cupboard beneath the counter and was pouring tea.

"I hope tea is fine. I can make coffee. Or water?"

"Tea is good."

Stacy carried the cups to the table near the window. "I'd rather sit here, if you don't mind."

"Not at all." Daphne put the cookies down and sat. "There's sugar and milk if you want. And please have a cookie. Did you have breakfast?"

"No. I had an orange juice when I spoke to Rupe but when he didn't believe me either... I crawled back into bed and had a cry. Of all people, he should believe me."

Of all people? Interesting.

"Is it possible he seemed to not believe you because so far there's no evidence to support you?"

Stacy looked straight at Daphne, cup halfway to her lips. "You don't support me. You were there but somehow have forgotten what you saw." It sounded a lot like an accusation. "If I hadn't just heard you take Audrey to task, I would have thought she'd got to you. Made you change your story."

"Nobody has that kind of power over me, Stacy. If I had seen a body, I would say so but all I remember is Rupert's jacket floating in the fountain. Can you tell me exactly what happened? Why were you even out there?"

After taking a sip of tea, Stacy put down the cup. "I'd better not say. It was a silly idea, stupid really. I just always hoped, and I thought the time was right... but anyway, I was out there. Around the time I reached the tennis courts I realised I wasn't wearing my glasses and they weren't in my pocket. I mean, I often take them off when I'm just walking or not having to read anything, but I do need them. So, I started back to the hotel but heard something."

"What kind of something?"

"Like a cry. Not someone crying. But like someone had a dreadful shock and cried out. It was a man. I'm pretty sure, anyway."

"Did you go to see?"

Stacy nodded. "I called out that I was coming and ran toward the sound and didn't even consider it might not be a good idea. But when I got to where the sound was, up in the English garden, it was quiet. No people or noises. And I noticed the fountain wasn't bubbling or anything which I thought was weird. Anyway, I still hoped... well, I can't say why but I had a reason to wait at the fountain, so I did."

Meet me now if you dare.

Had she been waiting for someone for a secret rendezvous? Was Stacy hoping to meet up with another guest but accidentally slipped her note under the wrong door?

"What did you find at the fountain?" she asked.

Tears welled up in Stacy's eyes and Daphne got up to collect a box of tissues.

"Here you are, dear. Take your time."

Speaking of time, she had to either cancel the day spa appointment or leave soon.

Stacy blew her nose with a muffled 'thanks'.

"I was looking at the sky hoping the clouds would go away so I could see the stars. But from the corner of my eye, I noticed something in the water and had the most dreadful shock to see Rupe's jacket. The one he'd worn at dinner. I thought someone had thrown it in there as a prank but when I reached for it, I felt something under it. Something firm. And then there was a hand beneath the surface."

"You saw a hand?"

Well, this changed things.

"Yes. For an instant before the jacket moved with the water and covered it. I was so shocked I sat down and then you found me." Stacy raised her hands to look at her outstretched fingers. They were shaking. "It was a male hand. Thicker fingers. I guess if I only saw it for a second then you wouldn't have. I'm sorry."

"Would you like a cookie?" Not sure what to say, food seemed the best idea. Her own stomach was churning but not from hunger. There was more to this mystery than met the eye.

Stacy shook her head then stood. "I'm going to my room to think. Audrey has wanted me gone from the association for years and this time I think she'll find a way. I got the feeling Rupert was cross with me and that is unbearable."

"Here's my phone number." Daphne found one of her business cards and handed it to Stacy. "Anytime, dear, just call me. I am about to have a neck massage but if you need me and I don't answer, leave me a message."

After opening the door, Daphne checked the hall in case Audrey was waiting but there was nobody in sight. Stacy stepped out and her mouth dropped open.

"What's wrong?"

"Um. Er. Nothing." Her eyes went from Daphne to Rupert's door. "Thank you for being so kind to me."

She turned and hurried away.

An odd response. Had Stacy just put two and two together? If she'd meant for Rupert to get the note and mistaken the suite numbers... well, well, well.

Although she was worried about being late for her appointment, the chance to speak with Col arose as Daphne exited the hotel. He'd just finished a conversation with one of the guests and smiled as she approached.

"Mrs Jones. Feeling okay after the late night?"

"I am, thank you. And you can't have had a lot of sleep, between being woken to search the grounds and then up early for a second sweep."

He nodded. "Feeling tired but it's just part of the job."

"I wondered if you know when the police are coming."

"Police?" He scratched the top of his head. It was impossible to see his eyes behind his black sunglasses, but he finally nodded again. "They remember the last false alarm with Stacy Chester and asked if we believed her. I don't. And my men and I have spent a couple of hours out in the bush as well and there's nothing but her drunken ramblings. And the bottle of champagne she took with her."

"So, nobody is coming to speak with her. Or me?" This didn't sound right at all.

"I expect someone will be along at some point, but it isn't a priority."

"Well, perhaps it needs to be. Stacy saw a hand in the water."

With a heavy sigh, Col removed his sunglasses and rolled his eyes. "She never said that to me. I'll call the police station myself, but I think she needs her eyes checked."

"She wasn't wearing her glasses at the time, but even so, a hand is quite a shocking thing to see in a fountain." At least he was going to follow it up. These things were best left to the police. No need for her to poke around.

"Hello and welcome again, Daphne."

Maisie looked fresher than Daphne felt, considering the night they'd had. Tiredness was beginning to slow her down, but she'd managed to get to the day spa with a couple of minutes to spare. It was terribly humid now and dark clouds were looming in the distance.

"Did you decide between hand and neck massage?"

"Neck, please. It is feeling tight."

"Well, follow me and I'll take care of that. Not surprising after all the goings on during the night!"

In no time, Daphne was face down on a massage table after changing from her dress into a towel to give Maisie access to her neck and shoulders. The room was softly lit with the same pastel colours as the reception area. Scented candles added to the sense of peace and relaxation. If only she had an hour. Or two.

And no worries.

"Comfortable, Daphne?" Maisie asked as she warmed some oil

between her hands. "I'll have you out of here all calm and happy and in time for the next session."

As Maisie began to work on her neck, Daphne closed her eyes. The next session was a panel discussion about best practices and ethics. Surely ethics included how one presents themselves in public, particularly their dealings with other people. Even though Audrey was not a celebrant, she was married to one, was vice president, and through her bridal business was an important part of the wedding industry. Deliberately seeking out Stacy to revile her in front of her peers was far removed from ethical behaviour. At least to Daphne.

The half hour flew as Maisie's fingers worked their magic.

"I'll head back out now so you can dress but come and collect my little care package before you leave."

Almost back in her dress, voices from the next room drifted through the wall. Two women were discussing the scene Audrey made.

"Was embarrassing to watch. Stacy won't stand up for herself and we all know Audrey can be a right so and so when it suits her. At least she had someone looking out for her."

Another woman tutted. "What a mess, Joan."

"Exactly. But this Daphne Jones woman didn't take any nonsense from Audrey. Quite impressive."

A little surge of pride brought a smile to her face, and she zipped up her dress as the same voice continued.

"Pity about her baking skills, though," Joan said.

"What do you mean?"

"She took it upon herself to bring homemade cookies to morning tea."

"Well, that is sweet of her."

"You have no idea. They were awful."

Awful?

Tears prickled at the back of her eyes as the women burst into laughter. She shoved her feet into her shoes, put her glasses on, and grabbed her handbag, smoothing her hair in the mirror. Her face was red, and she noticed she was holding her breath.

Awful. First Audrey and now this woman said so. Her cookies were awful.

She somehow managed to smile and say thank you to Maisie, who gave her a paper carry bag to take back to her room.

And once she was in her suite, she stood there, in the middle of the living area.

What to do?

If two people hated her cookies so much, then perhaps everybody else did. They might have spent the lunch break comparing notes about how bad they were. About her baking skills or apparent lack thereof.

"How can I do this? How can I go back?"

Even as the tide of despair washed over her, she hurried into the bathroom and took off her glasses. She wasn't going to cry. And she wasn't going to take this to heart. Not without further investigation.

"You are strong, Daphne Jones," she told her reflection. "You have a good heart and a clever mind. You care about others. And you deserve to treat yourself with respect."

All true.

"And Stacy has it much harder right now so instead of being afraid of what other people think, go and show her how to hold her head up."

All good and well to give herself a pep talk but this was upsetting. She'd made cookies for years. Decades. All based on her own mother's recipe. Those cookies would appear anytime something was wrong, such as during the arguments between her parents. A plate would suddenly be on the kitchen table and the children would help themselves and find a quiet spot to hide until the adults calmed down.

The palms of her hands hurt. Her fingers were so tightly curled that her nails dug into her skin. Drawing in a long breath, she straightened them. Funny how an old memory can still affect you after all this time. She breathed out, repeated, and then found her glasses.

"John loves you. And he loves your cookies."

She smiled at herself until the sadness lifted. She splashed her face with some cold water. Glasses back on, she poured some water and drank it before reapplying her lipstick. It was time for the next session.

ELEVEN
STORMY WEATHER

Overhead, the sky had darkened as storm clouds rolled in. John hurried up packing to leave. Nobody wanted to be out here when the weather changed even if the tents were secure. More than secure, they were downright comfortable. He'd never slept in a proper bed inside a tent, but these were large, permanent structures and had all the bells and whistles.

His backpack done, he checked he'd left nothing behind and made his bed. He knew someone would come along and change the bedding before the next intake of guests, but he couldn't walk away and leave a mess.

At the entrance he turned back for a final look. Much as he'd missed Daph, he wasn't going to lie about how much he'd enjoyed the past twenty-four hours. Fishing in a fantastic river at his own pace. Taking photos of the river as well as a beautiful, secluded clearing he'd found, filled with native flowers. And the meals. Relaxed around a campfire eating what they'd caught, perfectly cooked by one of the guides, who happened to be a chef.

"Hope you had as good a time, doll."

Outside, the other men had gathered as they waited for the all-clear to leave. He joined Ted, who'd become a friend on the trek up here. They'd fished within sight of each other and then swapped stories over dinner. John had no doubt they'd keep in touch between their camaraderie and their wives being celebrants.

"This is my fifth trip here and I reckon this was the best," Ted said. He was married to the club's treasurer, Gloria, and talked about her all the time. "Now all we need is for those girls of ours to decide to come back again and we can begin a new tradition."

"I reckon next time I'd want a few days up here. Would love to show Daphne the clearing I found and go for some bushwalks. She'd get a kick out of the tent."

Ted grinned. "You really do everything together? And how long have you been married?"

"Fortysomething years. Daphne is a person who is easy to be around." John meant it. He'd met her at the end of high school, and they'd rarely been apart since. They never argued and always had each other's back, and he was grateful, every day, to have her in his life.

They set off a few minutes later in a line of sorts, between one guide at the front and one at the back. Did they occasionally misplace a guest? John almost chuckled aloud at the thought of how they'd explain losing someone out here. As middle-aged to senior men they were unlikely to take risks. Or wander far away enough to miss a meal.

Speaking of meals... already on its way to the hotel was a portable fridge filled with this morning's catches. These would be served as part of the gala dinner.

"Think we'll be lucky to get back before the rain." Ted caught up with John. "At least the conference is all indoors."

John glanced up. He wasn't worried about being out in it. But Daphne had a fear of storms. With luck, it would pass by without her noticing.

Going past the lunch table reminded Daphne she'd not eaten but there was no time now with Rupert holding the door open for her.

"Sorry. Am I late?"

"On time."

He closed the door and leaned down to speak quietly. Not that anyone would hear because attendees were still milling around and the chatter was quite loud.

"Stacy still wants to leave. She told me you were kind to her, and I thank you for helping her when Audrey was going off. I just couldn't get there in time to intervene." Rupert's forehead was drawn. He must feel he was right in the middle of this.

"Should she leave before the police speak to her?"

"I imagine they have better things to do than come all the way up here based on the drunken imaginings of someone who has done similar in the past."

Did he know about the hand?

"When is she leaving?" she asked.

"Unsure. She said she wanted to sleep for a while before the long drive back, so I've asked Mandy to put one of the drivers on call for later this afternoon."

"Is there anything I can do to help?"

Rupert's face creased into a smile. "My dear lady, you've done more than most of the association and yet you are our newest member. I would like to think you can now enjoy the remainder of the sessions and then the dinner without another thought about the unpleasantness of the past few hours."

Unverified bodies. Angry vice presidents. Cookie haters.

"I am looking forward to this evening, and to introducing you to John."

"You will both be at my table. Ah, looks like I'm required." With that, Rupert made his way toward the small stage, clapping his hands. "Find your seats. Starting in two minutes."

Daphne returned to her earlier seat, aware of a few glances in her direction. Whether it was about cookies or Stacy, she didn't know. What other people thought was not her business so she made herself comfortable and got her notebook out. This was a brand new one she'd purchased just for the conference. She did love a nice notebook.

The panel discussion turned out to be serious and even a bit on the boring side. Rupert and Gloria were joined by Nancy, who was a retired business lawyer and was a bit hard of hearing, so there was much repeating of questions. The only time ethics was mentioned was regarding overbooking of clients.

Fortunately, this was a short session, and the next one began as soon as the stage was cleared. Much more interesting was this masterclass on writing beautiful ceremonies no matter the occasion. There were step by step formulas, ways to use emotive words, how to involve one's clients in writing the ceremony, and several examples of unique ones. Daphne scribbled in her notebook as fast as she could, not wanting to miss a word.

The speaker finished to loud applause and Rupert joined them on stage. But he didn't get as far as saying anything before a long, deep rumble of thunder rattled the windows.

A few people squealed and then laughed.

Rupert spread his arms out. "What a grand entrance I make."

More laughter.

But Daphne wasn't laughing and gripped her notebook against her chest. John was out in this. His tent would be no protection. Or what if he was on the way back? The terrain was rough and a tree might get hit by lightning.

The lights dimmed then came back. Then went again.

A flash of lightning was followed by the patter of raindrops.

"We might take a short break. Let's meet back here in fifteen minutes and hope our power is restored."

That suited Daphne and she was on her feet and first out of the double doors. Not waiting for the elevator, she scurried up the steps, dragging on the railing, as more thunder rumbled. The rain was heavier with every minute and as she let herself into the suite, a huge flash of lightning hit something close by and she screamed.

From the living room window, the scene was wild as trees bent against a tirade of wind. In the distance, the storm forked lightning into the flat ground below.

She rushed to the bedroom and peered through the French

doors. The rain was like a sheet but through it a line of people emerged from near the tennis courts, hurrying toward the hotel.

"John!"

From the bathroom she grabbed some towels and remembered to pick up her key as she left the suite. What dreadful weather to be out in. But he was almost here and that made her feet fly down the stairs.

Front doors held open by staff, the returning men burst into the foyer. All were soaked to the skin, but they laughed and began to clap each other on the back.

You're safe.

John grinned at her as he shrugged off his backpack. Hotel staff were fussing around with towels, and she carried hers across to him.

"Hello, love. You look like you fell in the river. Rupert warned me you might."

"Rupert did? Not very encouraging."

"I told him you wouldn't."

"Knew you'd have my back."

Water dripped down his face and his clothes stuck to his body, but nothing was going to stop Daphne landing a kiss on his lips.

And then she handed him the towels.

The lights came back on.

"Looks like I have to go, John. You said you'd want a shower, but I thought you meant in the suite, not outdoors."

"Taking care of the environment."

"Here's my key. Yours is in the suite." She couldn't resist another quick kiss. "I'll see you in under an hour."

"And I promise to be dry by then."

People were returning to the conference room. The storm was easing. And John was back. Everything in Daphne's world was better again.

TWELVE
AFTERMATH OF THE STORM

"One of the vehicles is missing."

Daphne's ears pricked up at a conversation between staff at the reception counter. She slowed down. The conference could wait a minute.

"What exactly do you mean by missing?" It was Mandy speaking, her back to the foyer and her hands on her hips as she faced another uniformed woman. "And whose vehicle?"

"Cherry's. She went down to the carpark and hasn't returned."

"Why did she go there? We have no guests coming in today."

The other woman shrugged.

"Can't we raise her?"

"Not so far."

Daphne stopped, pretending to check her phone for something.

Mandy sounded worried. "When did she leave? I hope she didn't drive down during the storm?"

"Col said it was around lunchtime. He wants to go to look for her."

"Not until the storm has cleared. Can you please find him for me?" Mandy turned and picked up the landline phone. "I'll see if any of our contacts in town can check the carpark for us."

Not wanting to be caught eavesdropping, Daphne headed for the conference room.

Almost at the doors—which were closed—she remembered something and doubled back. Mandy was on the phone and made eye contact with a brief smile.

"I'm sure that's the explanation. And if you see her, would you give me a call?"

After replacing the receiver, Mandy smiled again, but she looked worried. "How can I help?"

"I couldn't help overhearing about the missing 4WD and I remembered seeing one of the cars leaving earlier."

"Oh, you did? Around lunchtime?"

"No. I was about to meet Rupert and Gloria for breakfast, so it was before eight. Closer to seven."

Mandy's brow furrowed and she reached for a book with 'Staff Communication' written on the front.

"Well, that is odd." She flicked through the pages then ran her finger down to an entry. "This was last night and is written by Col when he returned from the carpark for the final time. Our staff write down where, when, and why they use a vehicle, and he's said... returned to garage at eleven in the evening after the guest failed to show. Note with contact details left on carpark gate should guest arrive later. Gate locked and security activated."

"Isn't that late for a guest?"

With a nod, Mandy closed the book. "And unusual."

A missing guest. Who became a body, perhaps?

There was that little tingle of anticipation in her stomach. Could this be part of the mystery?

"I imagine a guest not arriving is a bit of a worry. The roads aren't the best and driving late at night..." Daphne left the rest to Mandy's imagination in the hope of more information. She crossed the fingers of one hand between her body and the counter.

"His wife mentioned this morning he'd had to cancel joining her at the last minute. Anyway, thanks for letting me know about the time you saw the shuttle. There'll be an explanation."

"I'd better get back to the conference."

Daphne knew she'd missed the beginning of the final session, but this information might matter. One never knew when a snippet of something would be a clue to solving a case.

No case. No clues. Stop sleuthing!

She managed to get to her seat without disrupting the session. Audrey was at the podium and for a moment, Daphne wished she'd skipped this one. After the earlier nastiness, she'd lost all respect for the vice president. But leaving would draw attention and she wasn't about to give Audrey the satisfaction.

"Our wonderful association has been a support system for celebrants for over a decade. As one of several organisations of likeminded people in a rapidly changing world, we understand the importance of providing more to our clients. Ceremonies which are a cut above. Memorable events which everyone around those involved will talk about for months. Offering more."

Audrey paused and gazed around. Her eyes met Daphne's and her lips puckered for a minute before she continued.

"And by more, I refer to holding ourselves to a higher standard. Our reputation as an association and as individual celebrants reflects on us all. If we step outside the boundaries of our profession, then we let everyone down."

She turned a page on the podium.

"An example would be a celebrant who fails to arrive at their appointed ceremony in a timely manner. Or one who overrides the wishes of the client in favour of their own beliefs."

She directed an unpleasant smile at Daphne.

"And most of us would never involve ourselves in matters that were not our business, or attract the attention of the media from our actions. Would we?"

The long pause stirred the audience and some turned to see who Audrey stared at.

Heat rose from her neck to her forehead. Everyone was looking at her.

"Audrey?" Gloria spoke from one of the front seats and Audrey shuffled whatever papers she had in front of her.

"We are fortunate to have the services of a capable treasurer in Gloria Long, who has held the position for a... *long* time." Audrey giggled at her own poor attempt of a joke. "The association's finances are in good health so the committee has supported an idea of mine which will help us all."

You could resign.

She forced her shoulders to relax. Her fingers to unclench. Her breathing to deepen. There was something seriously not right about the vice president and Daphne had an idea of what might be prompting the scathing comments.

Was it Darren who didn't arrive late last night and you don't know where he is?

"Imagine if we could offer our clients a broader range of services than just a ceremony. If they can go to your website and see floral displays and honeymoon destinations and hire cars and wedding venues, then you become far more to them than someone officiating on their special day."

"Some of us already recommend local supplementary businesses, Audrey. So, what's different about this?" a person called out the question.

"I'm pleased you asked. Let me ask you all a question first. What do you get from putting somebody else's business on your website or passing their details on to a client?"

A few people murmured to each other and another spoke. "They send clients to me so it's a reciprocal arrangement."

"So, you send business to them, and they refer business to you?" Audrey had both hands on the podium.

She was an impressive woman when she wasn't being mean. Apart from her immaculate presentation she had a confidence about her which gave weight to her words. She'd changed her attire since this morning and wore white pants and a matching jacket over a lilac blouse. Her earrings were now gold hoops.

"Then I am so sorry I didn't put this idea forward earlier

because you have all been missing out. Imagine how much money a florist makes from a wedding or a funeral? Or a function centre? And you?" She laughed shortly. "Celebrants are underpaid as it is, but you are throwing money to these peripheral businesses for a pittance in return."

More chatter, louder, which seemed to be what Audrey wanted for she waited with a slight smile. After a minute, she held a hand up, palm forward, and the room quietened.

"There is a better way. Imagine getting a small percentage of every successful referral. Possibly a set amount. All for doing what you already are when you refer clients to another business. And not just wedding related. What about limousines or accommodation for bachelor parties and hen's nights?"

The original speaker stood up. It was a young woman with bright red hair. "Audrey, I'm sorry to interrupt, but this feels a bit... I don't know... distasteful. And too commercial. Speaking for myself, I refer to businesses who I personally know and can wholeheartedly recommend and I'm not going to go to them demanding a fee for doing so!"

"Perfectly fine for you, or anyone here, to continue as is. But as you rightly stated, you are speaking for yourself while I am speaking for the association you belong to."

Gloria coughed. Twice.

"Is this some money grab from the association? Because I won't remain a member if so." The younger woman's tone was sharp.

Rupert, who'd sat quietly off to one side of the stage, climbed to his feet. "Jessica, I can assure you this is not a money grab. And although Audrey has the committee's support to discuss this concept today, it isn't approved as yet. The last thing I'd want to see is you, or any of our members, leave, so please hear Audrey out. All members will be contacted in a week or two with further details and a survey and I promise our involvement will only go forward if the majority want it."

Jessica sat. Rupert stayed on his feet, moving to lean against a wall.

Audrey glanced at him and raised her eyebrows before taking a sip of water.

"Apologies for any misunderstanding. I'll give you an outline of what I envision. I think it is fair to say I am well known and regarded in the wedding industry, and I have many, many contacts across the different businesses which come together to create someone's dream wedding. My intention is to create a hub, if you like, filled with photographers and travel agents and function centres... you get the drift. They'll be broken down by region and that is where you all come in." She held her arms wide open. "You will have your own page on a central website, all beautifully set out, with complementary businesses local to you having something like a calling card on your page. Oh, I really wish I had a mocked-up page to show you, but my laptop didn't arrive last night."

Did Darren have it? If so, no wonder Audrey was so agitated. It might have nothing to do with her thinking the worst about him and Stacy and everything to do with not having the full presentation materials for the session.

"Nevertheless, this hub is on its way to reality, and I am offering all of you the opportunity to get in at the very beginning. The association, assuming this is approved, will pay a one-off fee which will allow members to have their individual pages on it for an initial free year, followed by a heavily discounted rate to continue."

Jessica stood again and there was a flutter of giggles and a couple of groans. The young woman cast a glare at those laughing. "This hub of yours. It is going ahead with or without us?"

"Yes. The website is under construction and there is a lot of money about to be invested into making this a nationally recognised resource." Audrey spread her arms apart. "It will be a virtual wedding expo and *the* place to be."

"You've not explained why we should have a page there. And why should we have these businesses on our page who we may not have any knowledge of, or affiliation with."

"Every time your page results in a successful connection you'll receive a finder's fee. You'll make a passive income to use however you wish."

"For a few dollars it isn't worth risking your reputation referring to somebody who might have poor business practices," Jessica noted.

Audrey laughed. "Few dollars? No, precious. You'll start at low three figures per referral and the sky is the limit considering how many moving parts there are for each ceremony. The wedding industry is far more lucrative than you know, and it is about time you started exploiting it."

Daphne reached the top of the stairs but before getting to the corner to the lounge area, she stopped and flattened herself against the wall out of sight.

Gloria and Rupert were talking, and it was about Audrey.

They'd left the conference room the second the session ended. People were crowding around Audrey asking question and she was smiling and nodding. Jessica had also rushed out. Poor Jessica. They'd never spoken but it was clear she had strong feelings about how she ran her business and wasn't a fan of Audrey's approach.

"Well, I wish he'd arrived. If nothing else, you and I could have looked at this model of Audrey's before the session and got her to approach how she shared the information differently," Gloria said.

"I phoned him yesterday when I got here to wish him luck with the wedding he had on. He was sweating on her laptop finishing some massive update so he could pack it and seeing as he disagrees with most of Audrey's plan, I imagine him being here would have created more friction." He made a scoffing sound. "As if we need more friction. Audrey is on thin ice in my books."

Thank goodness they are paying attention. Poor Stacy needs all the support she can get.

"She's taken such an odd dislike to Daphne and I'm not at all sure why. Daphne is so nice." Gloria's words were a surprise.

"Yes. She's a sweetheart and I won't have any further digs at her by Audrey. I think it is time—"

Footsteps stomping up the stairs interrupted whatever Rupert was going to say. Daphne coughed and emerged, digging around in her handbag.

"Oh. Hello. Just looking for that key and then I remembered I gave it to John when he arrived back from the fishing trip. Soaking wet! Did you see your Ted?" she asked Gloria, aware she was babbling.

"I didn't know they were back. Excuse me." Gloria smiled and went in the opposite direction to Daphne's suite.

Other people wandered past from downstairs, and Daphne waved to Rupert. "Better go check on John."

"See you both at six."

Yes. Yes, they would. At least being in the same room as Audrey wouldn't be so bad now John was here.

"Champagne ready to open. Glasses chilled. Fruit sliced. Chocolates being chocolates." John checked off his list. "My clothes are ready. Ah, need to get my shoes out."

On his way to the bedroom there was a tap on the door.

"It's only me."

John opened the door. "There is no 'only' about you."

Daphne grinned and headed for the living room while he closed the door. "Oh my! What is all this, love?"

"I hoped you might join me in a pre-dinner drink?"

She dropped her handbag onto a chair and reached her arms out for a hug. "Sounds wonderful. And much needed."

"Missed you." He had. And he'd missed cuddling her. He squeezed her until she giggled and then he kissed the tip of her nose.

"We have a lot to catch up on but if you can give me five minutes, I have something to do," she said.

"Take as long as you like getting ready. We have just over an hour."

After wiggling out of the hug, Daphne went to her handbag and pulled out one of her notebooks. "Getting ready will need to wait. I have a few notes to record before I forget."

"In that case, shall I pour us a glass of champagne?" John asked.

"Indeedy." She sat at the table and rummaged in her bag for a pen. "There you are."

While he opened and poured the bubbly, she had her head down writing. He carried the glasses over and handed her one with a 'cheers'.

"Cheers. Mmm... nice."

She put down the glass and gave him a funny look. One he recognised. Something had happened during the night, this much he knew. A false alarm about a body in a fountain from a person who'd had a bit too much to drink. Surely in the short time he'd been away she hadn't found herself a mystery.

He sat opposite. "You're not making notes about the conference."

"You know me too well."

There were worry lines around her eyes he'd not noticed when she came in. She caught at her bottom lip with her teeth, and he reached his hand across the table to take one of hers. "Tell me everything."

This made her laugh at least and she closed the notebook.

"I can offer an abridged version given the short time window we have." She glanced outside. "At least the weather has cleared."

The storm had passed as quickly as it began and only the glistening trees gave away the recent downpour.

"You sent me a text message about a missing body. Somebody in a fountain. Don't tell me you've found the body?" he asked.

He loved Daphne with all his heart and would do anything to help her, but lately they'd been involved with several mysteries around weddings and funerals. The last twenty-four hours was a delight without anything to worry about except which spot to stand in to fish, or whether to have dessert.

She shook her head. "No. We found Rupert's jacket in the fountain. It is red and made of velvet so easy to identify. And by we, I mean Stacy Chester found it—she works for the association, managing the membership and most of the administration side. But she'd left me a note under the door, and I saw her leave the hotel in the dead of night so I followed and—"

"Whoa. Hang on a sec. You followed someone in the middle of the night? What note?"

"Here." Daphne slid it out of an envelope on the table. "I'm pretty sure Stacy wrote this, but she denies it."

The poem didn't make much sense apart from being an invitation of sorts.

"This was under your door, but she says it isn't hers?"

"Well, she's not seen it. But she told me she didn't know which room is mine and then earlier today, after Audrey upset her, Stacy was here and had a moment when she noticed Rupert is in the next suite. I have a theory."

"And my head is spinning, doll. Can you go back to the fountain?"

Daphne outlined what she thought she saw and then what Stacy claimed to see. How she wasn't certain there was more than the jacket in the water and Stacy's claim someone moved the body. No wonder Daphne was keeping notes. This was right up her alley.

"And now I am concerned about the wellbeing of Darren Sutton. Audrey's husband. He should have arrived last night but didn't. So, what if it was him in the fountain? What if he did arrive but somebody killed him and then moved the body?"

"Didn't you say the hotel staff went out to search?"

"They did. Unless one of them is in on it. One of the hotel's 4WDs left this morning and hasn't returned." Daphne took another sip.

"Okay. We have no body but a guest who was a no-show. One alleged sighting of this body by someone who'd had a lot to drink. A search party finding nothing to back up her story *and* a history of her acting a little oddly up here."

"I wish I'd thought to take photos last night. And I didn't wake up until Rupert knocked to invite me to breakfast with him and

Gloria, so I haven't been back up there." She sighed and tapped her fingers on the glass.

John checked the time. "Feel like a quick walk? Rain's gone."

Daphne's smile made the offer worthwhile. Now to dispel her concerns and put the mystery aside.

She'd changed into sensible walking shoes, which looked a little odd with her polka dot dress but that was too bad. Most of the guests were probably preparing for the gala dinner and the hotel staff would have seen stranger attire than hers. They'd need to be back in about twenty minutes to allow changing and freshening up time. It was humid out here and steam rose from the path as the sun heated it.

"I'd already been to the English garden. After you left yesterday, I went for a lovely walk around the grounds and sat there for a while enjoying the peacefulness."

"The whole property is an interesting mix of natural growth, like all the gum trees and native flowers, and the manicured gardens," John said. "Even the hotel is a combination of styles which somehow works."

The archway came into view and Daphne slowed. What if there had been some poor soul in the water and she'd not taken the time to discover who it was?

"I came in this way through the hedges. And it was so dark because there was a heavy cloud cover and the moon only appeared every so often. I stopped here, near this statue, which gave me quite the fright!" She laughed. "Thought it was somebody standing there."

John said nothing. His lips were pressed together.

"In hindsight I shouldn't have come out here alone, love."

He glanced at her with a half-smile.

"And I wouldn't have, not just from the note. But seeing Stacy disappear into the dark and knowing she'd had a lot to drink... I couldn't have left her out here alone."

"Except you think the note was meant for someone else. For Rupert?"

"I'm drawing a long bow."

In the late afternoon sun, the water in the fountain sparkled.

"Still not working."

"Have you seen it in action?" John strolled around the base.

"Yes. It cascaded nicely during my afternoon visit. But last night I noticed how quiet it was and wondered if the staff turn it off at night."

"No need. See this?" He pointed at the top of the fountain. "On the bowler hat."

Daphne had to step back to see high enough. There were a couple of small, flat boxes facing up. "Solar panels. Like on top of Bluebell."

"Something may have come undone inside. You said there was a jacket in the bottom so there might be a blockage from it." John took his phone out and began taking photos. The fountain, including the water from different sides and angles. The statue. And around them both. Hedges. Statues. Benches.

"And Stacy came from which corner when you arrived with Rupert?" he asked.

"There." She pointed. "Col and another staff member said they had a good look but there was no sign of anyone, or anything to indicate recent movement. It all seems unreal now."

Phone away, John put an arm around her shoulder. "Must have given you quite a scare. Not sure I'd have kept my head."

"If you'd seen me running back to the hotel you might not be so kind. I was sure Rupert was dead in the fountain, but it was only his jacket."

"Which got there... how?"

An excellent question.

"Well, he wore it to dinner but we were all sitting outside on the roof and it was warm, so he took it off. He told me he must have left it there by accident so presumably, a person unknown picked it up."

"Why? Was it some prank?"

I am so glad you are back.

"He seems well liked. But this association has a lot going on under the surface." She glanced at the water. "So to speak. I overheard him say to Gloria that Audrey was on thin ice with him."

What was going on among the committee? Daphne had served on a few in her time and managed to stay clear of petty politics and power plays. But other people took themselves more seriously and in-fighting wasn't uncommon.

"We need to head back, Daph. I'll need some time to make myself beautiful."

"You are already beautiful, Mr Jones."

"Not nearly as lovely as Mrs Jones, though."

Hand in hand, laughing, they walked away from the fountain. A sudden chill shot up Daphne's spine and she glanced back. Nothing and nobody in the garden area.

Except she knew.

Someone was watching again.

FOURTEEN
DESSERT SURPRISE

On the way to dinner from their suite, Daphne gave John the lowdown on who was who. "Rupert is loud and kind and a bit eccentric. I really like Gloria. She's Ted's wife and the treasurer. Down to earth and nice. We're sitting with them, so Rupert told me. And hopefully Audrey will sit elsewhere."

"I take it she isn't the friendliest of people?"

"Unfortunately, she's taken a dislike to me."

John stopped them both. They were almost at the upstairs lounge area. "Care to elaborate?"

Daphne preferred people to make their own judgements rather than sway them with her point of view. She lived her life, giving others the benefit of the doubt. But this was different.

"Remember, I said earlier Audrey was upset with Stacy? Well, I was there and Stacy was afraid of her, so I acted as a bit of a buffer between them. I suggested it wasn't the place to have a go at Stacy, not with most of the other celebrants watching on and she got a bit... snippy."

Thinking about it made her blood pressure rise.

With a smile, John kissed her lips. "Always looking out for someone else."

They continued down the stairs.

"And what about Stacy. Is she alright now?"

"Not really. Last I heard she was going home before the dinner."

"Daphne! Daphne, wait up!"

Stacy ran to meet them.

"Scratch my last comment," Daphne whispered. "Hello. I thought you were leaving, dear."

"I would but there's storm damage on the road with a giant tree down and no access. Not even for the police coming up here. So, I've pulled myself together, dressed myself up, and intend to enjoy the evening."

Dressed up was an understatement with a fully sequined pantsuit and matching shoes.

She put her hand out to John. "I'm Stacy Chester. You must be John."

They shook hands.

"Are you going to sit with us?" Daphne asked.

"No, I'm not feeling welcome at the executive table. Might join Jessica and some of the others who aren't Audrey fans. Could use a bit of solidarity. It's been nice to meet you, John. And you look gorgeous, Daphne."

With that, she tore down the steps as though on a mission. Hopefully, it wasn't to find more alcohol.

"She's right." John took Daphne's hand as they reached the bottom steps. "You do look gorgeous and I'm so proud to be your date tonight."

"Aw. You'll make me blush." Her heart overflowed with love for this man. "And you are so handsome in your suit. I admit I've missed seeing you in it since we retired."

He leaned in. "Maybe I need to wear it more often?"

She giggled and squeezed his hand. John made everything good in her life. But she was quietly proud of how the dress she'd recently bought made her look and feel. Not quite floor length, it had soft, flowing lines and was blue—the same blue as the highlights in her hair—with a lacy bodice. A pair of heels and she was ready to dance.

The gala dinner was in the conference room and as they entered, she almost gasped at the difference a couple of hours had made. Set around a dance floor, tables of eight were decorated with candles and flowers. The stage was softly lit with a large screen rotating beautiful scenes of nature in time to low music. White aproned staff carried bottles of wine to the tables and the mood was festive.

A tingle of excitement pushed away all the other feelings and worries of the past day.

But a little thought niggled in her mind. Stacy had implied there was no way up or down the mountain. Exactly how long had that been the case?

As principal of Rivers End Real Estate, John had attended his share of conferences over the years. When he'd gone without Daphne, particularly when they'd been fostering children and she refused to leave them with anyone else, he'd learned what he could, networked, and been happy to go home without staying a minute more than required.

Tonight was different. This was her new world and she was shining. In the past few weeks, she'd been firm about walking more and eating less and although he loved her regardless of a few extra kilos here and there, she was keen to be healthier. And that was something he wholeheartedly embraced. He patted his own stomach which had flattened thanks to keeping pace with his wife.

A tall man with white hair on his shoulders stood and waved and Daphne led the way to his table. He wore a forest green velvet jacket and bowtie to match and wasted no time kissing Daphne's cheek.

"Don't you look divine, Mrs Jones." He held a hand out to John. "I'm Rupert Witherspoon and your lovely wife never believed for a minute you would fall in the river."

"Nice to meet you. And thankfully I managed to avoid such a catastrophe."

Ted and Gloria arrived, and introductions followed. Ted and John elected to sit next to each other to continue a discussion about fishing, and Gloria settled on the other side of Daphne, with Rupert next. There were three empty seats at the table.

"Hope you won't find this too boring, John," Ted said. "Lots of speeches between courses and then there's the awards."

"Awards?"

Ted gave him a look of disbelief. "Does nobody tell the newbies anything these days? There'll be awards for different categories. Best ceremony with heart. Or humour. You get the drift. All based on comments from clients who elect to fill in a short feedback form. Daphne will have left them with her clients."

He didn't recall her doing so. She was unlikely to do anything if she felt it might put someone out.

"We used to do similar with our real estate clients, not that Daphne ever called them a feedback form. I think it was a 'how did we do?' thing. And these are then voted on? Or how does it work?"

"Stacy manages them. She reads everything that comes into the association whether a feedback form or a legal letter. First point of call really and nothing gets past her. Be a pity if this little incident sees her out of a job."

John had no intention of sharing his thoughts on the matter. Not when he had so little information to go on. But he wasn't against listening.

Ted continued, "With the awards, Stacy makes a shortlist for each category and then the committee votes. She's the only one who knows the winner until each envelope is opened. Not even executive know who they've voted on."

"Makes for a fair result."

"It does." Ted glanced around as though to check nobody was close enough to hear. "But it also gives one person an awful lot of power."

· · ·

"Looks like we're missing two people." Gloria looked around their table.

"Stacy is over with Jessica. I don't think she's comfortable being here if Audrey is."

Gloria leaned closer. "Honey, if Audrey gives you a hard time, you let me know and I'll have a quiet word. She's upset about her husband not attending but that is no reason to act mean."

Audrey chose that moment to arrive, throwing herself onto the seat beside Rupert and launching into a whispered conversation with him. She'd changed again. Her hair was in soft waves around her face and her dress was black and floor length and tight in all the right places. Why she'd ever believe her husband would stray made no sense to Daphne. Audrey was a smart and beautiful woman. But she had shown an unkind side so who knew what their relationship was like? Living with somebody who wasn't your friend was unthinkable.

I'm so lucky.

She glanced at John. He listened intently as Ted regaled him with a story about a fishing trip in Tasmania and she had to smile. If nothing else, coming here had been good for him. He was supportive of her new career and never complained about longer than expected stays or sudden changes of plan.

"I should have just brought the thing with me, Rupert." Audrey no longer seemed concerned with being overheard. "Darren insisted he'd bring the laptop once it completed an update, but I think he had no intention of coming here."

"Last time I spoke with him he did. We planned a game of tennis tomorrow. And a swim."

"Yes. You two old fogeys enjoy wasting your time." Her words might have been on the rude side, but she smiled at Rupert and he grinned in return. "I'll remind him he missed out on beating you with his backhand and that there are less opportunities with every passing year."

Rupert threw his head back and laughed.

By now, Daphne was getting used to his easy-going nature and ability to laugh at himself. But Audrey confused her, as did her relationship with Rupert. They clearly had known each other for a long time and it seemed as though her husband and Rupert were good friends. Was the woman so stressed about her husband—or the laptop—that she was behaving out of character toward others?

Rupert, quickly followed by John, reached for bottles of wine from ice buckets scattered around the table, and began filling glasses. Audrey checked her phone and put it face down on the table before picking up her glass and sipping. Her eyes roamed the room, resting on Stacy who was drinking and laughing.

"Why didn't Darren join us, honey?" Gloria asked.

Audrey sighed dramatically and looked at her. "He said he was too tired to drive up. That was last night. Not even late. I suggested he reconsider because he would be missed and got the impression he'd changed his mind. But alas, he didn't."

"And you've spoken today? You must have wanted your laptop."

"I would love to have had the laptop, Gloria, but it doesn't seem to have made a negative impact. After my session I've been inundated with people falling over themselves to get in on the ground floor of my new venture."

Money talks.

"And what about you, Daphne? Are you going to join the fun?" Audrey said.

John jumped up and reached his hand across the table. "I'm John Jones. You must be Audrey Sutton? A friend of ours has one of your beautiful wedding gowns."

Audrey's mouth fell open and then she shook John's hand.

He sat back down, and Daphne put a hand on his leg and squeezed. How had he remembered Elizabeth White, their friend in Rivers End, had bought a Sutton gown for her upcoming wedding? Even she'd forgotten.

"Well, I'm most happy to hear that, John. Daphne, you should have told me."

I've been too busy protecting Stacy from you.

"I'm sure I would have got around to it." She turned to Rupert. "I heard a tree fell across the road down the mountain."

"Several, actually. And some of the road gave way. One of the hotel staff is stranded on the other side. I imagine there are plenty of people working on clearing and fixing the road for those leaving tomorrow."

"But we're every bit as stranded." Audrey contorted her face into mock fear. "Let's hope there isn't a real murderer on the loose up here." Her phone buzzed and she picked it up. As she read her message, her face didn't change, but when she put the phone down again, she shot a look of pure venom at Daphne. "Who told the police they saw a hand in the fountain?"

All talk at the table stopped and all eyes turned to Audrey. She appeared happy to have the attention—again. John put a hand over Daphne's, and she held back whatever she was going to say.

"Was this hand disembodied?" Rupert sounded amused but those worry lines were back around his eyes. "And is the hand responsible for tossing my expensive, and much loved, jacket into the water?"

"I'm not joking and as president you should take this more seriously," Audrey snapped. "The police are apparently attempting to get up here sometime tonight."

Gloria seemed unimpressed by the other woman's mood. "Why is this a problem? If the police are here, then they can investigate the strange events of early this morning. *They* are then able to remove any thoughts of foul play."

"Foul play? Are you some deluded fan of Agatha Christie? The only foul play was somebody thinking it funny to put Rupert's jacket into the fountain. Clearly it was all a joke, and I know exactly who did it." Audrey finished her drink and held the glass out for someone—anyone—to refill. "Little Miss Panic-Pants will do anything to get your attention back, Rupert. But she might have gone too far this time."

FIFTEEN
THE WALLS CLOSE IN

Rupert excused himself without responding to Audrey or refilling her glass. John did the latter, which kept her attention on him rather than Rupert, who had caught Stacy's eye and gestured, with a nod of his head, in the direction of the hallway.

Without a beat, she followed, and the door closed behind them.

What I would give to listen in...

"Daphne, would you care to visit the ladies' room?"

Gloria was already halfway to her feet and Daphne wasn't about to be left behind. If Gloria wanted what she did, then who was she to interfere?

"Be right back, love," she said to John.

It was obvious he'd seen what she had because there was a slightly pained expression on his face. But the corners of his lips turned up.

"Oh, maybe I should join you." Audrey reached for her phone.

"I was hoping you might tell me more about this new venture of yours," John began. "I'm a small business owner and love hearing about enterprising initiatives."

Last seen, Audrey had moved to Daphne's seat and was chatting to John. That should keep her occupied for a while. She went through the doors and Gloria grabbed her arm, making her jump.

"Shh," Gloria whispered. "I *have* to know."

Before Daphne could respond, Gloria had set off in the other direction. The hallways were long, with a few corners and 'Hotel Staff Only' signs on several doors. They reached an open door to the outside and the familiar smell of cigar smoke signalled Rupert's presence close by.

"There's a smoking area out here behind the screen."

Then Gloria was on the move again and Daphne had little choice but to follow. No point one of them being there alone.

"You do realise I'm more than forty years your senior, darling?"

Rupert's voice carried as they found a spot behind a tall bush. They couldn't see him or Stacy which hopefully meant they wouldn't be caught listening.

"Age doesn't matter. Only the heart," Stacy replied. "Anyway, I don't get your point. Audrey is out to get me so stop going on about a note."

"Might need to ask Daphne if we can see it again. It was dark last time I glanced at it. Because if it isn't your handwriting then of course we'll need to dig around and see who is behind this."

"I vote for Audrey."

Rupert chuckled.

"Is my job at stake, Rupe?" There was a wobble in Stacy's voice. "I really did see a hand in the fountain."

"I don't know. Once the police get here, we might get some answers but so far Col and his crew have searched high and low and there isn't a trace of a body. Now before you get upset with me, look at it from my perspective. You were in the English garden at the fountain where you believe you saw a dead body. You say you didn't write the note, so why exactly were you out there?"

A long silence followed.

Was Stacy working out how to dig herself out of a hole after denying her involvement?

"Look, I'm not comfortable discussing this, Rupert, but I promise you I did not put your jacket in the fountain. I'd never damage anyone's property, least of all yours. May I go back inside now?"

"I'll finish the cigar and be along in time to make the opening announcements. But, Stacy?"

"What?"

"Honesty is best. I know it is hard if feelings are involved but don't let that stop you standing up for the truth."

"It hurts me you think I'm not. Really hurts. Even last year nobody believed me about the missing laptop except for Darren." She ended the sentence with a sob and a second later her footsteps hurried inside.

"Oh, Stace..." Rupert murmured.

Gloria and Daphne exchanged a glance but before they could go, heavier footsteps went past in Rupert's direction.

"Ah, Colin. Any news?"

"Nah. Road is too blocked to clear in the dark. Can't even get around it with a motorcycle thanks to where the trees fell. Straight rock up one side and straight down on the other with a chunk out of the surface." Col laughed. "Couldn't pick a better spot to fall if someone wanted to keep everyone out. Or in."

"I see. Must make it difficult to remove the body before the police arrive."

Gloria and Daphne clamped their hands over their mouths at the same time.

Col stopped laughing. "Not funny, mate."

"Is it Darren?"

"Is what Darren? Do you mean Darren Sutton? Mate, he never arrived. Remember, it was me waiting for hours in the bottom carpark."

"I'm just stirring you up. Must have been a pain sitting down there until eleven at night and all for nothing."

"His no-show bothered others more than me. Housekeeping had his suite ready and one of the chefs was still up to finish the meal Mr Sutton requested. You want to stir someone up, find the chef. But it's just part of the job. And also, part of the job is locking the garage which is where I was going. Good night." Col sounded a little less annoyed than earlier.

There were no more sounds, just the occasional whiff of smoke. A tickle began at the back of Daphne's nose and she put her fingers on its end and squeezed. How would they explain their eavesdropping if she sneezed?

At last Rupert headed indoors and Daphne held her nose until she was sure he was gone.

"We'll give it a min and go back. Are you quite alright, honey?"

Daphne tested a sniff and all was good again. "Had the worst tickle thanks to his smoke."

"I tell him off about that habit every chance I get. He doesn't listen."

"Gloria, why would Darren Sutton have a separate suite to Audrey?"

"He's an insomniac. And, like Stacy, is a bit of a wanderer at night so might go for a walk at odd hours. He once told me when he got his pacemaker it messed with his body clock."

What if he was up at the fountain and something awful happened... but how did he arrive at the hotel if Col didn't bring him? And why would anyone hide his body?

"Let's get back before they send a search party. Rupert will wait for us because I have to announce one of the awards."

Awards?

But Gloria was already off at a faster pace than looked possible with her high heels.

There was a lot to consider. Pity she couldn't run upstairs and get a notebook.

Audrey was back in her own seat and Rupert was at the podium reading notes. John and Ted were again chatting, and nobody seemed to notice when Daphne sat and reached for her wine glass. On the other side of the room, waiters served entrees table by table.

Daphne rubbed her stomach when it growled. She'd had a

piece of fruit and one chocolate in their suite but nothing else for hours.

"Good evening to you all, celebrants and partners. Welcome to the gala dinner and awards night from your committee and executive. I'm Rupert Witherspoon."

There was a ripple of laughter. As if anyone didn't know the president.

"I see our entrees are being served so will make this quick. We'd like to extend our thanks to the hotel staff and management for once again creating a warm and comfortable environment for our conference. And to the committee, I wish to make my own special thanks for the hard work undertaken over the past year."

There was clapping until Rupert raised a sealed envelope.

"This is the first award of the evening. I'd like to ask our treasurer up to present it. Gloria, will you join me?"

More clapping as Gloria pushed her chair back and made her way to the podium with a wide smile. She accepted the envelope from Rupert, who took a few steps to one side.

"Look at you all! Isn't this a lovely evening in this lovely hotel? Well, because I can see entrees heading to my table, I'm going to hurry along and announce the winner of our fundraising category. As you know, each year we run a different effort and our most recent one was dear to my heart, being a wonderful raffle for prizes from Victorian chocolate makers. Yum. One person sold such a lot of tickets, and I'm pleased to celebrate their contribution."

She opened the envelope and slid a folded sheet of paper out.

"I love this bit because I have no idea who the winner is. Oh, and there is a lovely glass trophy on offer."

Gloria unfolded the paper.

"How cute. It appears to be written in a poem."

Even as Gloria drew a breath to speak, a premonition of doom clutched Daphne's stomach.

"There's no way in and no way out

No matter how you try

Before midnight there is no doubt

That one of you will... die."

The entire room gasped.

"No, but... what is this? Rupert?" Gloria handed the sheet of paper to him as he reached her. She fanned herself with the envelope.

Reaching for John's hand, Daphne knew this was from the original poet, if one wanted to be so generous. Or else someone able to copy a style. She glanced over at Stacy. She wasn't in her seat.

"Guests, please calm down." Rupert spoke over the rising talk. "This is clearly a joke. A very poor taste joke. Nobody is dying unless the author meant dying of laughter at such a lame poem."

"But what if there's a serial killer loose?" somebody called from a back table and a few people murmured in agreement.

"As nobody has died, how can there be a serial killer?"

Jessica stood. "Stacy saw a body in the fountain. That sounds like a murder victim to me!"

"Sit down, Jessica. Nobody wants to hear your theories." Audrey also stood. "What a ridiculous situation. Who gave you the envelope, Rupert?"

Jessica sat with a thump.

"All the envelopes are together in the box." He gestured to a shoebox sized metal box with a lock. The lid was open. "I was here when Stacy unlocked it."

"Well, what do you have to say, Stacy?" Audrey demanded, turning to look at the table where the other woman had been seated. "Where is she?"

People looked around.

"Jessica, when did you last see her?" Rupert asked.

"She followed you out."

"But after that?"

"You came back but she didn't." Jessica leaped to her feet and pointed at Rupert. "What have you done to her?"

SIXTEEN
FINGERS POINTING EVERYWHERE

The next few minutes were chaotic.

People yelling at each other from one side of the room to the other.

Other people crying.

And some running out of the room.

"Daph? When you said we'd have a relaxing weekend in the mountains, is this what you expected?"

They hadn't moved from their chairs, but Ted had gone to the podium to escort an upset Gloria back to the table, settling her beside him and getting her a glass of water while she continued to fan her face with the envelope.

"Gloria, dear? Perhaps we should pop that envelope into a plastic bag. In case the police need it," Daphne said in a calm voice.

As if it burned her fingers, Gloria dropped the envelope, which fortunately landed on the table. "Oh no, what if I contaminated evidence?"

"I'm sure you haven't. But you have had a bit of a shock."

"Stop mothering everyone, Daphne!" Audrey was still on her feet. "Gloria, what on earth possessed you to read that aloud? Look at what you've done."

Ted glared at Audrey. "I'll stop you right there, Mrs Sutton. Keep your nasty words to yourself."

Gloria kissed Ted's cheek, and he reddened.

"He's like you, John. Always the first to defend the woman he loves," Daphne whispered. "And this is not what I expected at all!"

The waiters, who had been about to serve their table, stood in confusion with their plates aloft. As bizarre as this situation was, there was no point in good food going to waste and John got up and had a word to one of the staff. In a minute, the entrees were in place.

"Excuse me. Is there any chance you'd have a zip lockable bag or similar? Big enough to put this envelope in?" Daphne pointed to the offending item. The waiter she'd addressed nodded and hurried away. "Do you think it is wrong that I'd like to eat?"

"Not at all. I'm starving."

The room gradually quietened. Rupert was off the podium talking to Mandy, who had hurried in at all the commotion. She shook her head and nodded and tapped on her phone.

The entrée—a mini tart filled with whipped ricotta—was delicious, all things considered. And the food was welcome, even if a few people gave them odd looks for eating. Gloria hadn't touched hers, but Ted's was long gone.

"How can you people eat at a time like this?" Audrey finally sat. "All this noise and anger."

"And nothing we can do until Rupert works out what is going on." Daphne pushed her plate aside. "I missed lunch, Audrey. And that was because I was on the receiving end of someone else's anger."

Well. Wasn't Daph doing well standing up for herself?

"Okay. I get the hint and apologise for being unpleasant to you. Stacy and I have a long history and I've been dreadfully worried about Darren, but you just happened to bear the brunt of it all."

"I accept your apology." Daphne smiled. "Have you had an update on Darren?"

"What? Oh, where he is? Well, I assume he went home but

we've not spoken since early yesterday evening. The reception is bad up here which is one of the first things I'll fix when I..." She clamped her lips shut.

He'd have loved to ask, 'when she did *what?*'.

Daphne wasn't as hesitant.

"Oh, are you moving here? If you buy the hotel, it would make the most wonderful place to run your new wedding hub from. Once you fixed the coverage up." She spoke with total innocence and a particular sweetness. Sleuth questioning mode activated.

Audrey had just taken a mouthful of wine and almost spat it out. After wiping her lips, she stood and picked up her phone.

"Who told you such a thing? Oh, never mind. Believe what you want. You and Stacy and Rupert. I'm about done with this silly little association."

With that she stormed out of the room, even trying to slam one of the doors in her wake. She was not given that satisfaction as the doors closed at their own pace.

Rupert climbed back on the stage. For a moment he gazed around the room, his face pained by whatever was going through his mind. John barely knew him but had the feeling this was a man who was genuine and cared about people. What a dreadful situation to be put in.

"Ladies and gentlemen, can I have your attention, please? Thank you." Rupert waited as a few people returned to their seats. "Thank you for staying. I understand a few of our guests tonight have chosen to remove themselves from the room and I will be going to find them and make sure they are doing alright. But I want to say how sorry I am, how sorry your committee is, that some unknown person has interrupted our special evening. Rest assured, I will get to the bottom of this. Now, I've spoken with Mandy, who you all know. Neither of us believe there is any risk to any of you, but she is contacting the police as well as getting all her staff involved."

His calm manner was working magic on many of the guests.

They visibly relaxed. Only a handful, Jessica for one, held themselves tightly and glared in his direction.

"As hard as it might seem, I would count it as a personal favour if each and every one of you remained here for our gala dinner. We have beautiful courses to come and much to celebrate. I promise you will be safe."

There was one comment of 'how can you promise that?' which was shushed by other guests. He'd won them over. That and the need people have for normalcy. Much easier to believe someone was playing a twisted joke than there was a killer on the prowl.

Waiters began clearing the entrée plates, which on some tables, guests frantically began to eat from. Normal talk continued. The music came back on. And Rupert returned to the table.

The first thing he did was push away his wine glass and swallow some water. Then put his fork on his uneaten plate of food. He glanced around the table, his eyes resting on Gloria, his mouth in a straight line.

"I'm fine, honey. Just gave me a shock," she said.

"I am so sorry."

"How is this your fault?" Daphne asked.

"You've seen firsthand how dysfunctional we are. I should have taken this more seriously. Where's Audrey?"

"Off in a huff," Gloria said. "I'm more concerned where Stacy is."

He nodded. "Agree. Are you up to keeping things going here while I look for them both? And see how the others are?"

Gloria looked down and Ted put a hand over hers. "Happy to take over until you return, Rupert. Pretty sure I remember how to keep people in a room."

Rupert and Gloria laughed. It made no sense to John and from Daphne's face, nor to her, but the mood lightened, and Rupert stood. "Thank you."

"We'll help." Daphne was up in an instant. "More chance of finding them all if we split up. Coming, love?"

If it would speed up the process of settling the guests down and bringing on the main dishes... of course he was.

No. She was not to blame for Audrey's outburst and subsequent departure. But still, she could have worded things better. There was a lot going on in the background and somehow the so-called body in the fountain was connected to this scare.

In the hallway, doors closed behind them, Rupert suddenly stopped and leaned against one of the walls, his shoulders slumped.

"Are you unwell?"

"Like Darren, I have a pacemaker. That's how we met. In a hospital twenty years ago. Unlike Darren, who is back to an almost normal life, I still need some medications to help things remain stable."

"Do you need something now?" John asked, putting a hand on Rupert's shoulder. "Happy to get what you need if you don't mind me going into your room."

"Thank you, but I have them on me. A glass of water, though?"

John went back into the room.

"I'll be alright in a few minutes. This stress isn't helping," Rupert said.

"At the risk of increasing your stress levels..."

Rupert managed a small smile. "You want my risk assessment?"

"I do."

"Someone is stirring up trouble. What better way than to create havoc at our premier event where we have most of our members present?"

"Any theories why? Or who?"

"None."

She didn't believe him for a minute. He knew these people better than anyone and must have some insight into whether the brewing storm between Stacy and Audrey was at tipping point.

Mixing your metaphors, Daph.

"What about Darren?"

"What about him?"

How to word this? "Audrey said she last spoke to him early last night. And thought he might have decided to join her after all. But then no contact. Is it worth checking in with him?"

Rupert took his phone from a pant pocket. He held it at arm's length and dialled. "Let's ask him where he is." The phone was on speaker and the number rang a few times before going to voicemail.

"I'm Darren Sutton and I love that you called. Leave your words behind and I'll listen to them all."

Rupert rolled his eyes. "Daz, it's Rupe. People need to hear from you. Call me."

"Leave your words behind?"

"I know. Terrible attempt at poetry."

They looked at each other. Then Rupert shook his head.

"Everyone who knows Darren teases him for his dreadful rhymes. But he didn't just threaten to kill someone and nor did he leave you a note to meet him at the fountain. He's never met you so even—*even*—if he had arrived here and somehow not been seen by his wife or all the other people who know him, why would he ask you to meet him at the fountain?"

"What if it was a mistake? My door? The note was meant for someone else, and the person got the room numbers wrong."

John returned with a full glass of water. "Sorry it took so long."

Rupert returned his phone to one pocket and pulled a small pill container from another. After swallowing a pill, he straightened. "Thank you. These won't take too long to work so I'll push on." He left the glass on the table outside the doors. "I want to see if Mandy has news from the police."

Reception was almost as chaotic as the conference room had been. Several guests were lined up and luggage was scattered around the foyer. There were staff behind and around the counter, some on phones and others trying to reason with the guests. Bits and pieces of conversations highlighted just how seriously some had taken the poem.

"We are so sorry but there literally is no way down the mountain until the road is cleared."

"I understand you are upset but we don't have access to a helicopter…"

"You have to call the army! Call the Premier! Anyone who can save us."

"How will you protect us? We need to lock the doors!"

Mandy hurried to them, stray hairs escaping from her normally perfect bun. "I don't know what to tell people. But I can't have them yelling at my staff so if there is anything you can do?"

"I'll speak in a minute. Anything from the police?"

"There are two officers who are going to walk up. They are waiting for a lift as far as the blockage from one of the emergency service workers, but it will take them a couple of hours to hike up here. We can't even pick them up partway as the road is too dangerous. They know we've had a written threat."

"Did they suggest any action to take?"

"To keep people calm. Continue as usual. Not let anyone wander around outside alone." She glanced over her shoulder to where one of the guests was banging on the counter with their hands. "But how do I keep them calm?"

Rupert clapped his hands until everyone was looking at him.

"I understand you're scared but I'm asking as your president, and as your friend, to take a breath. The staff are doing their best so treat them with respect. Please."

"But there's a killer loose!" a woman cried out.

"No. There's a note. A stupid joke designed to upset everyone. I'd very much appreciate you all standing up against whoever wrote that note by coming back to the dinner. Mandy needs a chance to speak to all of her staff to put a safety plan in place and this"—he waved his arms around—"is simply slowing the process."

Another woman pointed at Daphne. "This is your fault."

"Sorry?" Daphne managed.

"Audrey was right about us celebrants needing to stay out of other people's business, but you don't! You get involved and bring the police into it so of course you've got a target on your back and I just hope the person finds you and not an innocent bystander! If anyone deserves to die, it is you."

There was a shocked silence from everyone, guests, staff, and Daphne. John put his arm around her shoulders.

"Oh, what a load of rubbish!" Rupert almost bellowed. "Daphne has done nothing wrong so keep your nasty opinions to yourself, Joan."

So, this was Joan. Who hated her cookies.

"For that matter, we have a code of conduct which you've overstepped so I'll be wanting a word later on. This is quite enough."

One by one, the guests moved away from reception to congregate in the seated area. Although several cast looks of fury at Rupert, nobody challenged him. He winked at Daphne, and she took a few deep breaths.

"Thanks, Rupert," Mandy said. "I've asked Col to keep the team he's put together outside the hotel to make sure nobody goes in or out who doesn't belong here."

"Have you seen Audrey or Stacy?" Daphne asked. It was all very well calming the upset patrons but those two women, in her opinion, held the key to the strange goings on. "I'm happy to knock on their doors if you let me know their room numbers."

Mandy frowned. "Neither of them. Why?"

"Stacy hasn't been seen since before the, er, poem was read out. Audrey left soon after. We want to be sure they are both safe and sound," Rupert said. "Let's go and look upstairs. Mandy, can you let Col know to keep a look out for them?"

A moment later they were on the accommodation floor. Rupert went to the seats and dropped into one. "Bit of a racing heart. I'll be okay in a couple of minutes."

"Do you need medical attention?" John asked.

"Not at all. This happens now and then. Bad timing, though. Stacy is in room twenty-three. Audrey is in room sixty-six. It might be quicker if you split up."

"Not a chance," John said. "We shouldn't even be leaving you alone."

Now was not the time for being overly cautious. "I think Rupert is right. We're quite safe here, love. Within calling distance really. What if we take a room each and meet back here? And if we find the ladies, they can come with us."

Before John had a chance to argue, she was on the move. "Whose room is this way, Rupert?"

"Audrey. Sixty-six."

SEVENTEEN
BEHIND CLOSED DOORS

Daphne followed the hallway which headed to the back of the building. Then took a left. This was a dead end with four suites. The one at the end was sixty-six and there was no response to her knock.

"Audrey? Are you in there?"

Silence.

She tried the door.

Locked.

After checking nobody was coming, she leaned her ear against the door and although she counted to twenty, there wasn't a sound.

Next door was suite sixty-seven. This was the one prepared for Darren.

She tapped even though it was silly to do so, because he wasn't here in the hotel.

Of course, there was no response. She had better catch up with John. See if he'd had better luck. But first... she tried the handle.

The door opened.

Don't do it, Daph.

She pushed it wider. "Hello there. Anyone in?"

Silence.

It wouldn't hurt to look around. She closed the door behind herself, deciding against turning on any lights. Nobody was here.

So why was there a laptop bag on a chair?

Her bravery didn't extend to looking inside. And being in an unoccupied room was one thing but snooping around in someone's belongings quite another.

Her phone beeped and her heart jumped into her mouth. Or so it felt. But it was John.

> Any luck? No sign of Stacy so heading back to Rupert.

She quickly typed back.

> None. On my way.

There must be a simple explanation for the laptop bag. It might belong to Audrey and she'd left it in here for some reason. But she'd said Darren had the laptop. Unless this was a different one. Yes. That would explain it. Time to leave.

Under the door she could see the light from the outside hallway. And it was enough light to see an envelope pushed against the wall. Almost as if it had been dropped. Or pushed aside by a foot as someone came in and closed the door. It looked like the envelope from last night. The one slipped beneath her own door. Unable to stop herself, she picked it up. It was impossible to see if there was writing on it, so what to do?

"I cannot believe this is happening!"

Daphne shrank against the wall, even though the door to the hallway was closed.

Audrey was close by.

"Well, it means the police are totally involved now. Before it was all about Miss Husband Chaser stirring things up. Nobody believed her, not even that interfering wannabe sleuth."

Moi?

This had to be a phone call.

"Hang on, I'm looking for my key."

A couple of curse words were uttered.

"Once Stacy blabbed about the so-called hand in the fountain it became a problem we need to solve. You need to solve. Yes, that *is* what I mean."

The next sound was of a door closing.

Daphne waited. Listening and counting. When she reached one hundred, she let herself out after making sure the hallway was clear. She closed the door to Darren's suite with great care not to make a sound.

She straightened and released a breath.

The door to suite sixty-six flung open and Audrey stared at her.

"And just what do you think you are doing?"

"I might go find Daphne. As long as you are okay here?" John's worry level was rising after returning to the lounge area and finding only Rupert.

"Go right ahead. I'm feeling much better and will try calling Stacy again."

The elevator doors opened and one of the housekeeping staff stepped out. She carried Rupert's red velvet jacket which was in perfect condition. "Mr Witherspoon. I was going to hang this in your room."

"Would you mind? Looks as though you've given it new life."

"No more soaking it in the fountain. Fabric is dry clean only. And I kept the circle from the pocket." She took a plastic bag from the inside chest pocket and offered it to Rupert. "Thought it was a big coin but not so."

He frowned, turning the bag to see both sides of a flat disc a few centimetres across. "Not mine."

"It was in the pocket. I'll put this away for you." The woman left them.

"May I?" John took the bag. "I've seen these. Had a foster son who was obsessed with magnets." He held it near his watch which had a metal band, and it latched on. It took him more effort than expected to separate the items. "Strong as well."

"Would you hold onto it, please? Magnets are not friends of pacemakers."

"Of course. I'll be back shortly."

As John left, he slipped the magnet into his pants pocket. What an odd thing to find but if Rupert didn't own it, then there must have been a mix up in the laundry.

He followed the direction Daphne took, checking his messages again. The bars were down again so she might have had no reception. He should never have let her go off without him. Not that he believed there was a killer on the loose. Although that woman, Joan, wishing Daphne to be the target cut deeply.

Turning a corner, he found her. She was standing at the end of the short hallway sliding something into her handbag. Before he could call out, the door at the end opened with some force and Audrey emerged. Daphne visibly started.

"And just what do you think you are doing?" Audrey demanded.

"Hello, dear. I knocked and called but you didn't respond."

"But what are you doing at the door to my husband's suite?"

Daphne glanced at a door to one side. "That belongs to Darren? I was about to knock on the doors on either side."

What are you up to, Daph?

"What on earth for? Are you selling cookies?" The smirk on Audrey's face made John walk faster. "I'd suggest stick to being a retiree."

"Ladies." John slid an arm around Daphne's waist just as she stepped forward. "It is obvious you are safe, Audrey, so we will go."

"Since when is it the job of amateurs to look for criminals?"

Daphne wasn't budging but her whole body tensed. In a sweeter-than-sweet tone she smiled at Audrey as she spoke. "Since the criminals began to show themselves. Such an interesting way to describe yourself. Don't forget to lock the door." She glanced at John. "Shall we?"

The door slammed behind them as they left the hallway and once around the corner, Daphne stopped dead. "Oh my. That was too close."

"What was?"

She opened her handbag and showed him. There was an unopened envelope, somewhat crumpled and with part of a footprint on it.

"Daph..."

"I know. But I had to."

"But where? And how? I'm not sure I even want to know."

"Sorry. The opportunity presented itself. And thanks for rescuing me from Audrey. Did you hear her? She referred to herself as a criminal."

"Don't think she'd intended it to sound that way."

"Did you locate Stacy?"

"Not yet. Shall we go back to Rupert?"

But Rupert wasn't there. John rang his number and he answered.

"Back downstairs, John. There's been a... development if you and Daphne would care to join me at reception." His voice wavered.

"I heard what he said, love. But can we quickly open this? I know it's important. Very important."

Daphne plonked herself on one of the seats and gazed at him with a pleading expression. How could he possibly stop her? Besides, he was interested in the contents of this envelope.

Since the moment Audrey caught her in the hallway—or possibly from the moment she'd overheard the strange telephone conversation—Daphne's heartbeat was heavy and fast. Better not be the next one to need a pacemaker but at this rate, anything was possible.

She carefully opened the envelope and slid out a single sheet of paper, folded the same way as the one from Stacy. Or whoever was pretending to be Stacy.

"My theory is that whoever wrote the first note didn't mean it to be seen by me. I figured it was meant for Rupert. The way Stacy reacted when she noticed our suite is next to his made me wonder if she was the author, despite her denials. Now, I'm not so sure."

This note was simple. No map. No poem.

My secret love,

I made a terrible error by mistaking which room you were in.

We should be together. You'll be happier without her.

Will you forgive me and let us find our future?

S.C.

"Well."

They stared at each other.

"Indeed," John said.

"I thought Stacy was keen on Rupert. I even heard him remind her he is forty years older than she is, so possibly he is under the same impression."

"There seems to be a lot of catching up to do, Daph. Starting with where you found this envelope."

"In Darren's room. The one next to Audrey's, and don't look at me like that. It was unlocked and I was just checking Audrey wasn't in there upset or murdered or something. It was on the floor against the wall, so who knows how long it was there?"

Or who put it there.

"And there's more."

He sighed.

"Sorry, love. Audrey spoke to someone on the phone, and she told them to solve the problem. That was after mentioning—"

The beeping of her phone interrupted.

"Rupert again."

John stood. "Let's see what this new development is. Hopefully, something to do with dinner."

Oh, love. You haven't eaten in hours thanks to my wild goose chases.

"You must be starved. And isn't it the fish from your trip being served tonight?"

"Yes, and yes, but none of this is your doing. Well, apart from removing what may be evidence from someone else's room. And apparently getting intel about Rupert and Stacy... how exactly did you hear that conversation?"

A little less guilt-ridden, she took the arm he offered. "Gloria and I overheard them talking."

"Weren't you both going to the ladies?"

"Well. No. Gloria was deliberately going to listen in, and I had to make sure she didn't get caught. It was an odd conversation with Stacy denying she wrote the note and blaming Audrey. Says she's out to get her. And after she left, Col came along and he and Rupert talked about how bad the road was." What was it Rupert had said? Oh yes. "Rupert said something about how that must make it difficult to get Darren's body off the mountain."

"Huh? And you didn't think that was suspicious?"

"Rupert was trying to get a rise out of Col and managed it quite well. But there is a discrepancy about Darren. Col mentioned the chef was waiting on his arrival to make a meal for him, and Col had sat at the bottom carpark for a couple of hours. So, he was expected. Yet Audrey said she last spoke to him early in the evening and tried to talk him into changing his mind about coming."

There was something else. They reached the top of the stairs and started down.

"The first night here, I was sitting out on the rooftop with some of the others and Audrey made a toast to people who couldn't find their way up a mountain. She mentioned Darren and burst into laughter. That was after ten."

"Perhaps he called the hotel directly rather than Audrey? But it is strange."

Strange wasn't the word for it. Somebody or several somebodies was up to no good.

Rupert was at the foot of the stairs with Col and Mandy. His colour was better than earlier, but deep lines etched his forehead. "We've had some news. A bit disturbing, actually."

"Not about Stacy?"

"No. Although she seems to have vanished."

There was nobody else in the foyer now apart from staff. The guests had either retreated to their rooms or returned to the dinner and there was faint music drifting from the conference room.

Rupert continued, "One of the staff took a call from a resident of the local town. They've found a car which sounds like Darren's."

"His car?" Daphne said. Her stomach tensed.

"Looks as if it veered off the road and ended up in the river. They can't reach it to see if he's in..." Rupert dropped his head.

Daphne put her hand on his arm. Darren was his friend.

"There are emergency services heading there. Nothing indicates he's in the car. But the front of it is partly submerged. We all hope it isn't Mr Sutton." Mandy's eyes glistened. "He's such a gentleman."

Col tapped on his phone the whole time.

"Did Cherry make it back safely?" Daphne asked.

Everyone, including Col, looked at her.

"She left early this morning but I never heard if she returned before the road closed."

Col returned to his phone. "No need to worry about my wife. She's ex-army and tough as nails. Probably could move those trees with her bare hands."

Mandy managed a short laugh and nodded. "He isn't far off the mark. While we're on the subject of Cherry, I'd like to know why she left so early."

"Was close to lunchtime, boss."

"I saw her drive out before breakfast," Daphne said.

"You're mistaken." Col hadn't looked up from the screen.

"Col?" Mandy asked. "What was the purpose of Cherry's trip?"

He slid the phone into a pocket and gave Mandy his attention. "One of the guests she transported on Friday was carsick and she wanted to get to the carwash and do a proper clean before letting anyone in it again. Must have got the time wrong." His phone beeped. "We're checking the grounds for Stacy and I'm needed."

"Keep in touch, please," Mandy said.

Col grabbed a backpack Daphne hadn't noticed and dragged it over his shoulder, back on his phone as he strode away.

I'd love to take a quick look at his call history.

John touched her arm and when she glanced at him, he had a question in his eyes. Probably along the lines of 'what conclusions are you drawing from nothing?', or 'why don't you stop solving everyone else's problems?'.

"Solving!"

"Solving what, buttercup?"

Much as she needed to put a stop to Rupert's casual endearment, now was not the time. Not when he might be about to find out his friend was dead.

"Um... solving the mystery of baking better cookies."

That's what you come up with?

"Your cookies are fine, doll," John said with a frown. The frown might have been directed more at Rupert than her.

"Not according to Joan or Audrey. Both proclaimed them to be... quote, awful. I would love to speak to your chef, Mandy. When he or she is not in the middle of a banquet, of course."

"Um. Sure. I might check the gala dinner now everyone is back in there. Excuse me." Mandy hurried up the hallway.

Rupert took out his phone. "I'm going to try Stacy again. She needs to know about... Darren." With a small shake of his head, he dialled. It went to her voicemail which was merely a beep. "Stace, something's happened. It's about Darren and I'd rather tell you face to face. No more hiding. We need to talk."

Phone back in his pants pocket, he looked from John to Daphne.

"What is your take on all of this?"

"Mine?"

She'd not sorted a lot in her mind yet, nor gone through her notes with John. And there was a lot to take in.

"At some point you need to go back to the dinner and receive an award, Daphne. I saw the different comments from your clients, including one lady who said you'd put yourself at risk to bring her husband's killer to justice. And another whose friend had been buried in the wrong place, and you helped to work out where. People love you. Heart and mind."

Tears sprang into her eyes and she blinked fast. Had she really made such a difference? She knew who would have written those things but was stunned, particularly as one of them had been a main suspect of the police and had not made Daphne's time easy.

"I don't know what to say," she managed.

"Only what's in that sleuthing mind of yours."

Mandy approached, carrying a tray laden with plates and glasses. "Mains for you three. And sparkling water. Come on, I'll put this down for you."

They followed to where she set everything on a coffee table in a quiet spot and they quickly pulled chairs around it. The meal smelled so good that it took no time for them to each take a few bites of delicate fish in a creamy sauce and perfect morsels of vegetables. Simple but delicious. John finished his in no time but Daphne, although hungry, wanted to continue what Rupert had started, so she offered John the rest of hers.

She took a sip of water and dabbed her lips with a napkin, then settled back in the chair. "Not certain that my mind has a lot to do with this, but my gut leads me to make certain conclusions."

"I'm listening." Rupert pushed his own plate aside. "Please. Share your theories."

Stomach feeling much happier, John drank his glass of water, thankful for Mandy's thoughtfulness. The staff here were so lovely.

"Normally, I talk things through with John. It helps me sort out what is pure speculation and what might be based in truth. But everything is happening so quickly that I feel as if there are a hundred observations all vying for attention. So please, forgive me if I ramble."

Daphne clearly had lots going on in her head and was working on her unique type of magic: making connections which passed by other people. Certainly, by himself too often.

"I'll try not to bore you with what you already know so stop me if I do. In the space of thirty-six hours—actually, less than that—the following have happened." She held up one hand and counted her fingers. "Stacy says she saw a body in the fountain. One which subsequently vanished. Your own jacket was taken by persons unknown and dropped into the water. Audrey's husband was coming here, then not coming here, then coming here again. Except he didn't and now, I'm so sorry, Rupert, he may have been in a car accident. Meanwhile, Audrey comes gunning for Stacy, trying to rake up the past. Which seems an odd thing to do rather than let the dust settle. It isn't as though Audrey was involved in the events up at the fountain."

Daphne paused to drink some more water and for some reason, it reminded John of the photos he'd taken of the fountain. He wanted to take a look once they finished talking.

"A couple of times I've felt someone watching me," she said.

"Not that strange, is it? You are new to our association and have a reputation," Rupert suggested. "By reputation, I mean that people know something about you already."

"Daphne has a sixth sense about being watched. I've never known her to be wrong about it—and it bothers me she's felt it here. Can you elaborate, doll?" John was uncomfortable. If she was in any danger he'd lock and barricade them into the suite and stand guard.

"Out near the tennis courts and in the English garden. On the night Stacy was out there. It is the main thing which makes me believe she saw something. That and the notes."

Rupert straightened. "Notes? Plural?"

From her handbag, Daphne took the most recent envelope and the first one she'd found. She handed them to Rupert. "I'm going to confess I found Darren's suite unlocked and let myself in. That is where the second one came from."

All Rupert did was raise his eyebrows as his attention was on the notes. He read one, then the other, and returned to the first. With a heavy sigh, he handed them back. "That is Stacy's handwriting. I'd begged her not to pursue him, but she obviously wasn't going to listen to me."

"Age doesn't matter. Only the heart."

"How... Daphne Jones, were you listening to my conversation, my private conversation with Stacy?"

She nodded, biting her bottom lip, and her cheeks flushed. She was nothing if not honest but this time she may have gone too far.

Throwing his head back, Rupert laughed long and loudly. Even the staff behind the reception desk looked up in surprise.

"I'm really sorry I did. But I had it wrong, didn't I? I thought the note was for you and she'd accidentally slipped the first note under my door because it is right next to yours. But it was because she mixed up the numbers. Seventy-six instead of sixty-seven."

"I'd say so. She's had a thing for Darren for years and he hasn't helped. Always turning on the charm with her but I doubt it went further than that. I tried to remind her how old he is because I'm his age, but she didn't care," Rupert said. "And even worse was her butting into someone else's marriage, regardless of her believing Audrey didn't love him."

I kind of like you. Good morals.

"Do you think Audrey is capable of... um..." Daphne screwed her face up as she tried to sort her question out.

"Murder?" Rupert asked. "No. Look, I know you've seen the worst of her, but I've known her for more than a decade. Ever since Darren married her and I've known him twenty years. She is intense, granted. But one rarely is as successful in business as Audrey without being ruthless."

"But not ruthless enough to kill her husband."

As though the thought shocked him, Rupert shook his head rapidly.

Daphne was watching him, her fingers tapping against her leg. She had her thinking face on. Taking in data and processing it. John couldn't wait to talk to her privately and discover what she really believed.

From past the reception desk the sounds of the gala dinner increased as the doors were opened. A few people wandered out and one of the staff went to meet them, then led them in the opposite direction.

"They'll be going for a smoke," Rupert said. "Good that the staff are taking this threat seriously because even though I don't believe there's a killer at large, some of the guests do and this gives them some confidence. We work so hard during the year to put this conference together and I hate seeing anyone afraid."

"There's more," Daphne continued. "I overheard Audrey on the phone to someone telling them to solve a problem and she had just mentioned Stacy and the hand. I feel in my gut that there is something sinister at play, but what? She was upset the police are coming up here, but why?"

Probably it was time to ask the lady. And the timing was perfect for she had just emerged from the elevator and was briskly covering the distance in their direction. And she looked furious.

NINETEEN

ACCUSATIONS AND CONFUSION

"Daph? Audrey at your three o'clock."

John's words chilled her. There was no real reason why because he was here and so was Rupert as well as the hotel staff. But her last interaction with the woman was still fresh in her mind.

I'll keep quiet. Let the others talk.

"Rupert, we need to speak." Audrey planted herself where she could glare at them all. "Privately."

"Let me get you a seat. In fact, I insist."

John beat Rupert to it, probably as concerned as she was about his earlier heart issues. He placed another chair between Rupert and himself with a smile.

"Why?" Audrey demanded.

"I'll tell you in a minute."

With a huff, Audrey perched on the edge on the seat.

"What do you need to talk to me about, Audrey?" Rupert asked. "Would you like some dinner? I can ask Mandy to—"

"No, thank you. I want to complain about Daphne and would have preferred to do so without her listening in. I think you need to rescind her award."

I'm not going to say a word.

Thank goodness she'd only picked at her meal. Her stomach churned.

"This really isn't the time, Audrey."

"Make it the time, Rupert. She called me a criminal."

John leaned forward. "That isn't what happened."

"Of course, you will defend her." Audrey turned to Rupert. "Can't you see these people are here to stir up trouble? They have a track record of interfering wherever they go and look at this! Sitting here with you and no doubt lying about me."

Whatever are you covering up?

Although her heart was pitter-pattering too fast, Daphne was intrigued. Audrey was deflecting attention away from herself by attacking others. She'd done it with Stacy as well. So, what was she deflecting attention away from?

"Okay, Audrey. Time to stop you. I have some news, and it isn't good. I don't have all the details yet but there is a report that a car, which is possibly Darren's, is in the river down near the town."

Audrey's mouth dropped open.

"I'm sorry, darling, but there's no information yet about whether he is in the car. Emergency services are on their way there."

"But... how? It doesn't make sense." Audrey grabbed one of Rupert's hands. "He told me he wasn't going to make it here."

Time to say something. "But Col went down to the carpark to wait for him and the chef was still in the kitchen ready to make him a late dinner. Would he have let someone here know? Perhaps he couldn't reach you or wanted to surprise you?" Daphne kept her voice gentle.

A tear dripped down Audrey's face. Her eyes were wide.

"I thought he'd gone home after the wedding he officiated. He wasn't keen to drive up late even though he knew I was counting on it. Said something about his pacemaker feeling a bit off. It was adjusted a week ago and he's complained a few times. You don't think he... that the pacemaker..." Audrey took her hand from Rupert's and covered her face as a sob escaped.

"Hey... we don't know if he's even in the car." Rupert put an arm around Audrey's shoulders. "There should be news soon and in the interim, there's no point imagining the worst." He planted a kiss on the top of her head. "Time to stop being angry at Daphne and blaming Stacy for all manner of things. What if we all go back to the dinner for a while? Both of us have presentations to do and it might help if we show ourselves."

"This is my fault. I made him feel bad about letting me down."

"That is silly. Darren makes his own decisions. How about you go freshen up and meet us back at our table inside? If you don't feel like presenting, I'll do it." Rupert released Audrey. "Okay?"

She nodded.

"I'll tell Mandy where we are if she hears anything new. See you inside?" He got to his feet and Audrey stood.

"I'll be in shortly."

The woman who returned to the elevator was at odds with the one who'd stormed over. She walked with her head down and shoulders drooping. Despite her feelings about Audrey, Daphne's heart went out to the woman. Discovering her husband might have been in an accident was clearly a genuine shock. The tears were real.

Audrey could not have had anything to do with Darren's accident. If the poor man's pacemaker had failed in some way, it was purely accidental. How terribly sad this would be if it turned out he was in the partly submerged car.

More and more this was looking like no kind of mystery at all.

"And this concludes the awards for the evening. Congratulations to each and every winner and my personal thanks to those who worked tirelessly behind the scenes to make this happen." Rupert paused with a glance in the direction of the table where Stacy had been sat. She wasn't there and he continued, "Too many people to name, so please join me in one last round of applause. For us all!"

Daphne touched the glass award with her name etched into it.

Shaped like a wedding cake, it was for 'Outstanding Client Satisfaction'. She didn't quite believe it and intended to write to every one of the people who'd nominated her. Once she found out who they all were.

"Please feel free to stay as long as you like and dance the night away. The bar is still open. When you are ready to leave, one of the staff is happy to see you to your room." Rupert made to step down but once again, Jessica stood and waved her arms for his attention. "Yes, Jessica?"

"Oh, for goodness' sake. Would somebody put a gag on her?" Audrey muttered loud enough for their table to hear as she helped herself to a glass of wine.

Jessica stepped forward onto the edge of the dance floor and for a silly instant, Daphne imagined her asking Rupert for the first dance. Clearly the events of the evening were getting to her and the idea of getting into bed soon was appealing.

"Earlier you stated that the death threat was some kind of joke, yet the staff are happy to escort us to our rooms? Are we being lied to? Is this threat real?"

The atmosphere in the room changed. For the last hour, with awards and speeches, and a yummy dessert, the guests had settled back into enjoying their evening. Or at least not looking over their shoulders. But Jessica's questions had people glancing at each other and an undercurrent of murmurs ran through the room.

"The staff are there to make sure everyone is comfortable and if that includes walking to your room with you and even checking under the bed, then they will." Rupert smiled. "I am joking about the last bit. Nobody is telling lies, but the hotel management has taken the poem, such as it is, seriously because it's their job to do so. State Emergency Services are working on clearing the road overnight and many of you will leave in the morning, fit and well."

"Only many? Not all?" someone called.

Rupert rolled his eyes. "I'm staying until Monday. Probably others, too."

"Have you found Stacy?" This was Jessica, now with her hands on her hips.

"Not yet."

The murmurs rose into a cacophony of voices and as one, Gloria and Ted joined Rupert. Audrey stared into her glass. Nobody could blame her for not being up to dealing with upset people when she had so much to worry about.

John leaned closer. "I understand the association wanting the dinner to go ahead but it seems to have divided people and increased their fear, being in here without answers."

"Not that anyone has any."

Gloria and Rupert conferred for a minute with Ted listening in, then it was Ted who took the podium. He held his hands out, a bit like a preacher about to pray, and the room quieted. Jessica stayed put.

"Friends. Can we agree this evening—apart from the ridiculous note—has been enjoyable?" Ted asked. "I know you want to. After all, how often do you get the chance to listen to my dad jokes?"

Half-hearted laughter and a few nods.

"Without doubt this conference has been our most eventful. A storm. Trees down. And someone trying to spoil the awards tonight. How about we enjoy some dancing and make it clear we aren't about to let anyone ruin our special night?"

Ted was an impressive speaker. Confident but not loud, and careful to highlight the good and minimise the bad. As people visibly relaxed it was obvious why Rupert had asked Ted to step in for him. The lights dimmed, a popular seventies dance track came on, and the first keen dancers took to the floor. Jessica didn't move and Gloria made her way through the gyrating bodies to speak with her. It only took a minute and then Jessica returned to her seat and Gloria joined Rupert and Ted as they came back to the table.

"I think I might have that glass of wine now." Rupert slumped in his chair and ran a hand across his forehead. "Thank you, Ted. And Gloria."

"They're frightened," Gloria said. "Same as I was. And Jessica is egging them on which is annoying. Best thing for us all is to shut things down in an hour and let people lock themselves into their suites. Might give them a sense of control and security."

It was all surreal. Watching people dance and laugh while outside of this room, a tragedy was unfolding. She didn't want to be here anymore, among the tables and music. She wanted some fresh air and quiet and a chance to think.

"Feel like a walk, doll?" John asked.

"Mind reader. Yes, please." She reached for her handbag as John stood and picked up her trophy.

"You're not going?" There was alarm in Rupert's eyes.

"We'll take the trophy back to the room then I might show John the view from the roof. I'm only a message away."

"Okay. Yes, of course. But just... well, take extra care."

Daphne planted a kiss on his cheek. "We will."

He grinned and nodded.

The music changed to a ballad and as they left, Gloria and Ted were heading for the dance floor. Rupert had moved next to Audrey, and they were deep in conversation.

John took Daphne's arm as they left the elevator. She'd said nothing since leaving the table when he'd sensed she'd had enough of the artificial environment of forced enjoyment back at the dinner. He certainly had.

"How good is this trophy, doll?"

Finally, a real smile from her.

"And well deserved, Daph."

"I wouldn't go that far," she said. "While it was lovely for people to nominate me, I'm only memorable because of the bad things which happened to, or around them. If those things hadn't happened, nor would this trophy and I'd rather their experience with me had been less exceptional."

"Don't agree. They may still have nominated you, without the peripheral events."

As they neared their suite, Daphne located her key. "I'm beginning to feel as if I attract negative events. This is three terrible occasions in the past few months when people have died or gone missing. No wonder that woman blamed me!" Her voice quivered with emotion and John gently took the key from her.

"Time to get you inside, my sweetheart." He unlocked the door and held it open for her. "I might make us a cup of tea."

"I'll be right... back."

Daphne hightailed it to the bedroom and then the bathroom door clicked shut.

With a sigh, he set the trophy down on the counter and prepared tea. He missed Bluebell at this moment. Their teapot and cups. The quiet of the caravan's interior. What a peculiar weekend this had become.

When Daphne emerged, he had tea ready and was sitting at the table near the window. Her eyes were brighter than normal, but she smiled. Knowing her, she'd freshened up and given herself what she referred to as a 'pep talk' by reminding herself of her good points. Of which she had many.

"Sorry about before." She sank into the seat. "All got a bit much for a minute."

"Let's sit for a while and enjoy our tea. I've missed doing this."

"No tea up at the river?"

"Plenty. But no Daphne." He grinned.

"And no Daphne-related problems!" She frowned. "I'm not being down on myself, love, simply stating a fact. There are some problems here and one way or another, I can't be like the other guests and not do something."

"The other guests didn't have a note slipped under their doors."

"True. But I don't know if any of that meant anything."

John didn't understand. "Any of what?"

"The note. Or notes. The fountain. Even Stacy disappearing. I'm wondering if it was all about getting attention. Either to or from something else."

"I'm listening."

TWENTY
IDEAS AND CONCLUSIONS

As it was, they decided to venture onto the roof to talk. The tea was nice, but Daphne longed for fresh air and although the balcony would have done, showing John the rest of the hotel was something she'd been looking forward to doing.

The hallways were quiet.

As they waited for the elevator the music from downstairs drifted up.

Out on the roof, she drew in a long breath of the night air. The restaurant was still open, and she recognised a small group sitting around a table as members of the association.

"I wonder if they got as tired of all the accusations as we did," she said.

"Or they are planning a coup. Some pretty serious conversation going on."

He was right. There were three couples and one person was taking notes as another waved their hands about during an animated discourse. "Well, if they are, good luck to them. Rupert and Gloria are steady at the helm and I wouldn't be voting anyone else in. Some of the others, though..."

She led the way to where she'd sat the other night. Was it really only twenty-four hours ago? So much had happened.

No wonder I'm exhausted.

For her body, this was true. But her mind refused to quieten down.

They leaned against the brick balustrade. Here, it was peaceful and the air was warm enough to be comfortable. For a while they gazed out over the grounds and then wandered to the other side where the view, during the day, would be breathtaking. Lights from the local town twinkled a long way down.

"I wonder if they've got the car out of the river," John said. "Terrible thing to happen."

"It might take a while. With the SES trying to clear the road, who knows how many spare units there are? For that matter, shouldn't the police have arrived by now?" It had been more than the hour or two expected for them to hike up.

Lightning flashed in the distance.

"I'd love to capture that." John reached for his phone and drew his hand from his pocket with a frown. "Oh. Forgot I had this."

It was a round, flat magnet.

"Where did you find that, love?"

"Housekeeping found it in one of Rupert's pockets when they cleaned his jacket."

"The red one?"

"Yes. Said it was in his top pocket," John said.

"But that would affect his pacemaker. Well, maybe it isn't strong enough, but why would he risk such a thing?"

"He didn't. Asked me to hang onto it because he didn't want it near him. He's careful of his phone as well. Keeps it away from his chest."

How odd.

"You take some photos. I'm going back to where I sat last night to see if I can remember some things."

"I'll come with you."

"There are plenty of people up here so take your time. I won't go anywhere." She appreciated his concern but had no intention of prowling around in the dark or going anywhere she shouldn't. Once he nodded, she returned to the table and stared at it.

"Rupert was here. Stacy was there. And me."

She sat in the same seat. From here she'd seen Audrey toast Darren for not finding his way up the mountain so she must have had a call or message from him to say as much.

Stacy had gone in search of another drink and been disappointed. But she'd not been gone long.

Rupert's jacket had been on the back of his chair.

She went to the elevator and looked back. He'd been leaning against the balustrade staring into the night. His jacket was still on his chair when she'd left.

"Daph?"

"I'm here."

They met halfway.

"I was thinking about Rupert's jacket and remembered it was on the back of a chair when I left with Stacy. He'd stood up to look at the grounds below. Audrey and the people she sat with were at their table but almost everyone else was gone. I think the restaurant was pretty much closed as well."

"Are you thinking he accidentally left his jacket here and someone took it?" John still held his phone. "Shall I take some pics of the roof?"

"Could have used you last night." With a smile, she slid her arms around his waist. "I wouldn't worry now."

"Which reminds me... I want to upload the photos from the fountain to the laptop. Too hard to see the details on this screen." He planted a kiss on her lips. "Have I told you how beautiful you are? I love what you do for this dress."

"I love you, John Jones." She kissed him back. "We need to come back here when there isn't a conference."

"Couldn't agree more."

There was a noise... voices. Yelling.

They rushed to the balustrade and peered down. Trudging along the driveway on foot were two figures. One of them struggled beneath the weight of a large bundle in their arms. No, not a bundle. A person.

Staff ran from the front of the hotel, flashlights darting here and there as they covered the distance.

"Are those police?" Her eyesight wasn't what it used to be, but she was certain the figures wore police jackets. And yes, police belts and backpacks. "Who are they carrying?"

John had his camera trained on them, zoomed in as close as possible. "You might want to take a look." He held the phone on the police.

It was a woman, her head against the chest of the officer, who looked utterly exhausted but kept her gripped tight in his arms. One of the staff reached him and they transferred her to his arms. Her face—covered in mud and eyes closed—was there on the screen for an instant. And the glittering of the parts of her clothes without mud confirmed it.

Daphne gasped.

"Am I right?" John asked.

"That is Stacy!"

They took the stairs to the foyer, reaching there as the police officers arrived with the staff. The man with Stacy went to one of the sofas and carefully placed her on it while the officer who'd carried her looked around. He was filthy from head to foot.

Mandy pushed a stool from behind the counter with a quick, "Sit. We'll get you to a bathroom to clean up momentarily."

Daphne dropped to her knees beside Stacy and brushed the muddy hair back. "Stacy, dear. It's Daphne Jones. Can you hear me?"

"She's been unconscious since just after we found her, ma'am."

The other police officer squatted next to her.

"I'm Constable Leon Finnegan. Leon. Is there a medical officer or the like here?"

Mandy overheard. "On it!" She sprinted away.

"Where did you find her? What happened?"

Leon was young. Early twenties. His partner, who still looked wiped out, wasn't much older.

"Are you related to this lady?" Leon asked.

"No. But I know her. Stacy Chester. Oh, John, would you find Rupert and Gloria?" She took Stacy's hand. "She's icy cold. Can we get a blanket?"

"That would help. We had to cut through dense bush to get around the fallen trees and we heard her calling for help. She had fallen and hurt her ankle. We were almost at the top so came here rather than try to descend with her, but the ground was pretty rough."

Mandy returned with blankets and towels. "Someone is coming. We have an ex-nurse on staff. Along with a handful of the staff she went to rest, to swap with some of the others later on. With all this chaos and worry..." She handed towels to both police officers. "There's an empty staff room which we'll show you to. I think we can loan you both some dry clothes and get housekeeping to look at yours. But at the least you can go and dry off. Take a shower if you want."

Leon straightened. "Thank you very much. I'll stay here for now, but Constable Patterson would appreciate a chance to clean up."

"If you'd like to come with me, then?" Mandy led the way, the other officer casting an eye behind him as his footsteps left a trail of mud.

Daphne got to her feet to cover Stacy with a blanket. Leon's phone rang and he moved away. "Sorry. Haven't had reception until now."

Rupert and Gloria ran across the foyer with Ted and John behind them.

"Oh my goodness, honey, look at you." Gloria tutted. "Poor girl."

"She doesn't seem hurt other than an ankle."

"Then why is she unconscious?" Rupert pulled up a chair to sit near her and like Daphne had, he took Stacy's hand.

"There's a nurse here who is coming to help." Unsure what else she could say or do, Daphne stepped back. She wasn't part of the close friendship between the three but already cared about them.

What was Stacy doing out in the bush?

Leon returned, his phone still in his hand and his face serious. "Would one of you be able to take me to Audrey Sutton?"

Oh no.

Rupert's head shot up. "Is there news about Darren?"

"Er, there is. But I should speak with her first."

"He's been my close friend for two decades. He was in the car. Wasn't he?"

All eyes were on the young constable. "I'm terribly sorry. A body has been removed from the vehicle matching his description and with his driver's licence on their person. Pending formal identification, it appears Darren Sutton is deceased."

"Nooo!"

Stacy sat bolt upright, her eyes wide as she threw off the blanket and snatched her hand from Rupert's.

Gloria dropped her head.

Rupert slumped back in his seat.

"I'll find Audrey," John said. "I'm sorry to hear this." He hurried away.

"Thank you, Leon." Poor chap. So young to be breaking bad news. Police might be trained to handle these times, but they were people as well.

He nodded and made his way to the reception desk.

"It's all a lie. He isn't dead." Stacy clenched her hands into fists. "She killed him."

It can't be both.

"Stacy, you need to rest," Daphne said. "We thought you were unconscious. Hurt."

"I am hurt. My ankle. And my... my heart!" Stacy burst into tears, threw herself down, and covered her head with the blanket.

With a small grunt, Rupert got to his feet. He glanced at the form of Stacy on the sofa, his lips in a straight line. Then, he hugged Gloria, his eyes meeting Daphne's over her shoulder. Tears filled her own eyes at the pain in his. What a dreadful way to end what was meant to be a celebration of the association he presided over.

Audrey and John arrived at the reception desk and Leon spoke to her. There was barely a sign of grief at the news. She kept her head high. Her shoulders back. Only her hands, which rubbed up and down her crossed arms, showed anything was amiss. John stood close by. Such a caring man to be there even for a person who'd shown herself to be rude and unkind.

"I'd better speak with Audrey." Rupert released Gloria, who wiped her eyes on a handkerchief. "What do we do? About everyone else?"

"Not get them involved. They can find out later," Gloria said. "I'll ask Ted to wind things down. Send them all off to bed and put this... horrible day behind us."

"I'll stay with Stacy."

"Are you sure, Daphne?"

"Go and do what you need, Rupert. And you, Gloria. We're fine."

"Not fine." Stacy's words were muffled.

"I know, dear." Daphne sat where Rupert had. "Why don't you sit up so I can help you clean up a bit?"

Rupert and Gloria left while they could. Audrey ran across and threw herself into Rupert's arms.

"How could she?" Stacy had emerged and glared at Audrey. "This is her doing."

"Here's a towel. How bad is your ankle?" Noticing her voice had a sharp tone to it, she offered a friendly smile. "The police officer said you'd had a fall."

"I did."

"Whatever were you doing out in the dark?"

Seeing as Stacy hadn't moved, Daphne retrieved the towel and began wiping mud off her hair. After a minute Stacy took the towel back and cleaned her face as best she could without a mirror. "I don't know where my glasses are."

"Check your pockets?"

"No. I was wearing them when I slipped down the embankment. And I'm not about to go look for them so I'll need to get my spare pair." Stacy swung her feet onto the floor and winced. "Ouch!"

"The nurse will be able to help. Are your spares in your handbag? Actually, where is your handbag?"

"In my room. I only took my phone and key with me. Here." She pulled a key from her pants pocket. "I'm sure they're in my suitcase still. It's open in my suite."

"I'll only be a few minutes so please stay here. Don't disappear again, Stacy, we were all so worried about you. John will come and sit with you." Not waiting for a response, she headed toward the stairs via a quick chat to John to update him. He'd been reluctant to let her go alone but nobody else was free to watch Stacy and she promised to call if she ran into any problems.

As she stepped onto the first stair she paused, frozen by icy cold fear shooting up her spine to her neck, where the hairs all stood up. To look back would be to give away her knowledge to whoever watched her. Because she had no doubt somebody was.

Somebody with evil intent.

At the top of the stairs Daphne waited for a moment, listening. Was anyone following her? The sensation from before lingered. But who was watching her? Only the police officer was new, and it wasn't him. Everyone else she knew, even the staff. It was a mystery.

And there wasn't time to worry about it.

Key in hand, she located Stacy's room. Inside, it was smaller than the suite she and John were in but still had plenty of room with a main living area, a bedroom, and bathroom. No balcony. The room overlooked the single-story buildings belonging to staff.

The room was, to put it mildly, a mess. Clothes were left on the floor in both rooms and shoes were scattered around, not always in pairs. Half a dozen cups, some still containing coffee, were on the counter. And an empty champagne bottle sat upon the bedside table. Itching to do a quick tidy to help Stacy, considering her hurt ankle, she went as far as to pick up a top before stopping herself. Stacy might find it upsetting.

"Okay, let's find those glasses."

The suitcase was on the end of the bed, with a handbag beside it. Both were closed. Hadn't she said the suitcase was already open?

Inside were half a dozen items of neatly folded clothing. It was at odds with the lack of respect shown to the clothes on the floor.

"Hopefully, the room wasn't ransacked." It was only half a joke.

There was a slight lump beneath the bright yellow blouse Stacy had worn to the first dinner and taking care not to unfold the blouse, she slid her hands beneath the fabric and lifted it. The glasses case was underneath, and she juggled the blouse into one hand to put the case onto the bed. A handful of coins slid out of one of the pockets in the blouse.

Except... they weren't coins.

"More magnets?"

First there was one in the jacket of a man with a pacemaker. Who denied it was his. And here were more of the same kind. Tucked away in Stacy's pocket.

"Daffodils and ducks!"

She had to call John.

No. The police officer.

No. Take photos.

She opened the camera app on her phone and took a dozen images of the magnets, the blouse, and the suitcase. Then, she put everything back the way she had found them. Magnets in the pocket. Blouse neatly folded. Suitcase closed.

Careful to lock the door behind herself, Daphne slipped the key into a pocket.

The hallway was darker than she remembered. Maybe the lights were dimmed for the evening? She wasn't hanging around to check and picked up her pace even as she began to tap John's number into her phone.

As she rounded a corner, eyes on the screen, she ran straight into a chest. A man's chest.

"Whoa... slow down."

"Oh, Col. I'm sorry, dear. Silly me, typing a message instead of watching where I was going. Did I hurt you?"

"Nah. I'm tough. Did you take a wrong turn? I thought your suite was in the far corner."

"It is. I came to get St... something for someone. Are you here to check the lights in the hallway?"

He nodded but for an instant, confusion crossed his face. "Actually, I will check the lights but I'm also fixing a window. Mandy just dumped it on me so I'm going to do that before the guests begin leaving the dinner." He scowled and tapped the keys on his belt.

"Do you normally fix things?"

"I just do whatever Mandy tells me. She's the boss. At least for now." He started off again. "Gotta go. Watch your step around corners."

"Did you see Stacy is back? The police officers found her."

He turned back with a nod. "Good news. Not so much about Mr Sutton."

"Did you know him?"

"Met him a few times at conferences and when he visited with his wife a few weeks ago. I'd better fix this window before Mandy yells at me again."

Can't imagine Mandy yelling at anyone.

Col didn't like Mandy. Hadn't Audrey made some comment about some of the reception staff being difficult to deal with? What a shame to work in an environment you didn't enjoy. She'd been lucky almost her whole life to work side by side with John. Real estate had its moments, but never between the two of them.

"There you are." John was at the bottom of the stairs, his face lined with worry. "Everything go alright?"

"We have much to discuss. But first, would you mind taking these glasses to Stacy?" She held out the glasses case.

"What are you going to do?" John took the case.

"Offer my condolences to Audrey."

The other woman sat opposite Constable Patterson who had cleaned up and wore a mix of clothing. Audrey held a steaming cup of coffee. On the other side of the foyer, a staff member inspected Stacy's ankle.

"We'll keep you informed of any developments, Mrs Sutton," the officer said.

"Not that it matters now. It won't bring Darren back." Audrey glanced up as Daphne reached them. "I thought you'd retired for the night."

"Just running an errand. I want to convey our condolences for your loss. John and I are so sorry to hear about the dreadful accident."

Audrey blinked a couple of times in rapid succession. "That is kind of you both. Constable Patterson just told me he might have died before going into the river. There wasn't enough water in the car to have been the cause and there were no signs of braking on the road." She sighed. "His heart. He'd been telling me his pacemaker wasn't quite right and had an appointment with his specialist next week."

Unsure what to say, Daphne patted Audrey's shoulder.

"I'm sorry I said your cookies were awful," Audrey said. "Try adding more butter and a bit less sugar."

Now she really didn't know what to say. But Audrey had turned away to stare at Stacy, who was whimpering as her ankle was bandaged. She'd put her spare pair of glasses on and clutched the blanket like a lifeline.

John waited for her partway and just as she reached him, the doors to the conference room opened and people began to leave. He took her arm. "Shall we go outside while they disperse?"

It was good to leave the hotel, once they promised the staff member at the door that they'd stay in sight of the building and not be long. They walked for a couple of minutes and found a bench, where they sat. There was lightning in the sky again and it looked as if the storm was heading back toward them. After everything that had happened, Daphne couldn't muster up any feelings of fear about it.

"Audrey apologised."

"I beg your pardon?" John said.

"She did. For what she said about my cookies, and she even gave me a hint on how to improve them."

"I see. But they are great already, doll."

With a smile, she put her hands on either side of John's face. "They're not great. I still use my mother's recipe and never once questioned it. But I'm ready to move on and explore new ways to make them nicer. Much nicer."

Poor John. He was so supportive of everything she did and there'd been moments recently when she'd had the feeling he was being polite rather than telling her directly that she wasn't the world's best baker. His eyes gave nothing away so she kissed him.

"Thank you for loving me no matter what."

His face relaxed and he squeezed her in a warm hug. "It goes both ways."

Time to show John what she'd found.

What an amazing woman Daphne was. Always something new to surprise him and the revelation about the cookies was huge. How often he'd come up with a plan of how to raise the subject and then never did for fear of hurting her feelings. He remembered the cookies her mother made and somehow, she'd connected some dots and had made a decision to erase them. Another big step forward.

"I don't know where to start." Daphne nudged him. "Stop staring at the sky. We need to get to the bottom of this."

"Sorry. The bottom of what?"

"Do you still have that magnet?" she asked.

Funny thing to ask about.

But he pulled it from his pocket and held it on his palm for her to see.

"As I thought! You'll never guess what I found in Stacy's suitcase." She tapped on her phone. "First of all, her room looked like it was ransacked with clothes and shoes and coffee cups all over the place. But in her suitcase, where she'd said I'd find her glasses case, it was neat and tidy. She'd folded several items of clothing and when I moved one in order to retrieve the case, these fell out."

He took the phone from her and zoomed in on the image. "More magnets."

"Seven or eight of them. They were in the pocket of the blouse she wore the first night. The night she said she saw the body in the fountain."

Goosebumps rose on his arms.

"Let me get this straight. Housekeeping found a magnet in Rupert's jacket pocket. The jacket you saw in the fountain. And Stacy was there, wearing the blouse you just found more magnets in?"

Daphne nodded.

"Rupert is careful about protecting his pacemaker. I imagine anyone with one would have to avoid certain things which might interfere with it working, and it made no sense for there to be a magnet in his jacket pocket. Where are you going with this?"

"I honestly have no idea. I think I need to show this to the police, but I'd like to think she has a good explanation."

Daphne was way too kind. Raindrops landed on his head and he got up, extending his hand to her. "Time to go back."

On the way, she told him about seeing Col upstairs and his scathing comment about Mandy.

"Not easy to be in charge of something like this." He gestured to the hotel as they neared it. "All credit to Mandy for how she looks after the guests."

"It is a beautiful place. And would be ideal as a wedding and honeymoon destination but I wonder whether, with Darren passing away, Audrey will reconsider her plans."

Her plans? He must have looked confused because she gave him a little smile. "Earlier in the evening she started to say fixing the internet coverage would be one of the first things she'd do when... and then she stopped herself."

"Ah, yes. You asked if she was buying the place and she

stormed off. I thought at the time it was a peculiar reaction to an innocent question. But you don't know if that is her plan?"

"Not at all. Purely speculation. A gut feeling."

And Daphne's gut feelings were better than most people's careful calculations.

"And what is your gut feeling about Darren's accident?"

"I'm not ready to talk about it yet. I have some thoughts. And feelings."

Daphne was in full sleuth mode and if he planned on keeping up, he needed to pay close attention.

Once again, the foyer was almost empty. A few guests lingered, sympathising with Audrey. The two police officers, now both in mismatched but clean clothes, conferred with Rupert, Mandy, and Col at the reception desk.

"Shall we see if Leon is free?" John asked.

Stacy had pushed the blanket aside and sat with her feet on the ground, holding a glass of wine someone must have brought her. "Daphne, Daphne, you're back. Please sit with me." Stacy's voice wobbled and her eyes were red-rimmed.

"We can see when he's free from over there." Daphne wasn't about to miss the chance to let Stacy talk and when they got to her, she gave them a tiny smile.

"My ankle is okay. Just a bit bruised but it hurts. I hurt all over. And I have scratches down my arms from the bushes I grabbed at." She showed her arms. "This has been the worst night of my life."

And Darren's.

"I'm sure your arms will heal fast and your ankle. Is there anything we can get you?" She sat beside Stacy on the sofa and John took the chair which was still pulled up nearby.

"You've done heaps already. I'm sorry I hid under the blanket, but I was so shocked about... Darren. I can't believe he's gone because I always hoped..." Stacy spoke quietly with half an eye on Audrey across the room. "She doesn't even look upset."

"We are very sorry for the loss of your friend. When was the last time you talked to him?"

Stacy tore her gaze away from Audrey. "Oh. The other day." Her hand went to her heart. "He phoned to make sure I was attending the conference. So sweet of him. But before I could answer his phone cut out. He sent a text message to apologise once he went home. His battery had gone flat. Here, I'll read the messages to you." She opened her phone.

About to say it wasn't necessary, Daphne's gut told her otherwise with a small tingle of anticipation. Was she onto something which might help?

"I don't want you-know-who to hear. You read them to yourself." Stacy gave her the phone.

After exchanging a quick glance with John, she read the messages.

DARREN:

> Darn phone battery! Home now and charging up.
> What days are you there for?

STACY:

> Mine does that all the time. You can phone if you
> want. Arriving Friday and leaving Sunday. Or
> Monday. Depends.

DARREN:

> Better not phone you. Audrey is here working on
> the purchase offer for HHCR.

STACY:

> You still aren't keen on it.

DARREN:

> She wants me to sell my share portfolio to finance
> it. I'm yet to be convinced but am keeping an
> open mind because I love the place. Can't wait to
> be back there.

STACY:

You deserve happiness. A lot of happiness. 😊

STACY:

Still there?

DARREN:

Yes, darl. Gotta go.

STACY:

You busy man, you! See you Friday night?

DARREN:

See you there.

"See? He cared about me. And was feeling like he was being backed into a corner."

There was another message. One from Audrey.

She knew she shouldn't look. But she did.

AUDREY:

He doesn't love you. Or want you. He is pretending he's young again. Same as Rupert so stop chasing men old enough to be your father!

There was no reply from Stacy.

"May I have my phone?"

"Of course, dear. I'm such a slow reader. It sounded as though he planned to be here so do you know why he changed his mind?"

It took Stacy a minute to answer as she locked her phone and put it back into a pocket. "He didn't."

John was kind enough to find coffee for all three of them, although Stacy protested that more wine was a better idea.

Daphne glanced at her watch. Close to midnight. Outside, rain fell but there was little in the way of thunder or lightning. Perhaps it was waiting until she needed to go outside again. Her mind was working overtime and her body was wound up like a coil. Coffee was possibly a terrible idea, but it helped break up the moment to give her a chance to think.

Audrey wanted to buy the hotel. She was sure of that based on those text messages. And she needed Darren's financial help. It would be a big decision. But what really worried her was the message from Audrey. It was sent an hour or so after Darren's, so she'd discovered the conversation going back and forth. What did she mean by her reference to Rupert? Had there been something between him and Stacy after all?

"Here we go. Three coffees and some after-dinner mints." John put a tray down. "Stacy? I can ask for a meal for you."

She shook her head and then finished the last of her wine in two gulps.

John's eyebrows went up and down and he handed a coffee to Daphne with a small smile. He might not have read the messages, but he knew her well enough to sense she'd found something of interest.

"Stacy, dear. A few minutes ago, you said something about Darren. When I asked why he changed his mind about coming here you said he didn't. But he never arrived."

"Are you sure?"

"Not at all. But he was found deceased in his car outside the town down the mountain. And the mountain road has been blocked off since this afternoon. Not to mention nobody even saw him here and Col waited at the carpark to drive him up."

"You can't trust someone who has a reason to cover up a crime." Stacy popped an after-dinner mint in her mouth, her eyes back on Audrey who was on her feet staring back.

"We're getting company," John said quietly.

Rupert and Leon both had serious expressions. Well, Leon looked the way he'd done all along, but Rupert's face was... odd. Not the earlier grief. Nor worry. Was he angry?

"John, do you happen to still have the item housekeeping found in my jacket?" Rupert asked.

Daphne's heart sank. Something bad was about to happen.

John located the magnet and held it out. Stacy sipped coffee, disinterested.

Leon held a zip-lock bag open for John to slide the magnet into.

"Stacy, I have a question and you must be honest with me," Rupert said.

Her eyes shot up to his and she put the coffee cup down. "Anything, Rupe. You know I'd never lie to you."

"Last night you and Daphne left the roof together after we'd sat out there. Is it true you returned to the roof a little later?"

She did?

That would change a lot of things.

"Why does it matter?"

"Did you?" Rupert's eyes were intense, and his hands curled up.

Clearly, he didn't want it to be true. This was deeply upsetting to him.

"Yes."

Rupert's mouth opened and closed and he took a few steps away, turning his back on them.

"I only went to see if anyone was still there. Daphne didn't want to share her bottle of champagne or come for a walk so I thought I'd find someone else. But everyone had gone, and the restaurant was closed and in darkness. Why?" Stacy made to stand and flopped back onto the sofa. "Darn ankle."

Leon pulled up another seat and sat directly in front of Stacy. "I have a couple of questions."

"I'm very tired. Can't this wait until tomorrow?" Her voice had a whiny tone. "Daphne, tell them I need to sleep."

Daphne will do no such thing. She wants to hear the questions.

"When you returned to the roof and found you were alone, did you find Rupert's red jacket and take it?" Leon asked.

Stacy's eyes widened. "No! Of course not."

Out of the corner of her eye, Daphne saw Audrey inching closer as Leon continued.

"Did you place one or more magnets into the top pocket of Rupert's jacket?"

Rupert turned back around and Stacy gave him a pleading look.

"Miss Chester?" Leon pressed. "Did you?"

"No," she whispered. "Why would I have magnets?"

"Daphne." John was thinking what she was thinking. This wasn't how she'd planned to do this.

"May I interrupt?" she said. "I'm sorry, Stacy. I really am but I can't sit here and not show what I saw to the officer." After finding the first photo on her phone, Daphne handed it to Leon. "I intended to speak to you about this immediately, but you were busy."

He looked a bit puzzled but as he went through the photos, his face hardened. "Where were these taken?"

Deciding it was prudent to put a bit of space between herself and Stacy, she moved to stand behind John's chair and put a hand on his shoulder. His hand came up to cover hers, giving her the courage she needed to continue. "Stacy asked me to go to her room to find her spare set of glasses. I still have the key." She held it out to Leon. "She told me to look in her suitcase, which is where I found them. But they were beneath that blouse and when I moved it, all those magnets fell out."

"What magnets? Which blouse?" Stacy demanded.

Leon turned the camera to show Stacy an image of her blouse and the magnets. "These look the same as this one." He held up the plastic bag. "Found in Rupert's jacket."

Stacy's mouth opened and closed. Twice.

"Just what did you do, Miss Murder-on-her-mind?" Audrey butted in. "Did you try to harm Rupert?"

Head shaking from side to side, Stacy began to cry.

"Miss Chester, can you explain how those magnets got into your suitcase?" Leon handed back the phone.

"They're not"—sniff—"mine. I'd never hurt"—sniff—"Rupert. I love him."

Audrey laughed. "Sure, you do. We all know he had to tell you to stop following him around, turning up at his place uninvited, and making a fool of yourself. And that is when you latched onto my husband."

Leon looked at Daphne. "I'd like copies of these. Can you send them to my phone?"

She nodded and he handed her a card. Her hands shook too much, so John took the phone and card and did it for her.

"You need to fingerprint my room." Stacy brushed the tears from her eyes. "I'm being set up."

Maybe you are. But by who?

"Daphne had my key."

On the other hand...

"Stop it! That is enough, Stacy." Rupert's face was red and he raised both hands. "Don't blame Daphne. Or Audrey. Or anyone. I thought we'd moved past the unpleasantness last year to a place of friendship and respect so why would you try to kill me?"

"Kill you?"

"Magnets, Stacy. You know I have a pacemaker and that I don't even have my phone near my chest. The note under Daphne's door was meant for me, wasn't it? Trying to lure me out to your death trap and when I didn't arrive, you threw my jacket into the fountain and made up lies about a body." He shook his head. "Shame on you."

By now Stacy was sobbing and wringing her hands. She was either a good actor, distraught at being caught out, or innocent.

And I don't know which.

Col pushed a wheelchair over. "Mandy told me to bring this." He parked it and then kept walking, going through the front door.

Audrey moved it closer. "Hop in, Stacy. Makes it easier to wheel you straight to jail."

"Mrs Sutton, that isn't helpful," Leon said.

Rupert obviously agreed for he put an arm around Audrey's shoulders. "Come on. We'll find some brandy and make a toast to Darren."

They left in the direction of the conference room and everyone fell silent. Apart from Stacy's sobs. John took a folded handkerchief from his pocket—he had a habit of always keeping a spare—and gave it to her.

"Miss Chester, my partner and I would like to do a search of your room. We'd like you to be present."

Without protesting, Stacy allowed Leon and Daphne to help her up and into the wheelchair. "Daphne needs to be there."

"Why?" Daphne wanted to go somewhere quiet to think. Like their suite. In their four-poster bed. And sleep.

"Please."

"She'll need to stay in the hallway," Leon told Stacy as he took the handles and began pushing the chair.

She twisted her head to cast a beseeching look at Daphne.

"I'll be right up." It wasn't worth the argument.

John gave her a funny glance. "Not going up in the elevator?"

"I have a little job for you first."

TWENTY-THREE
HISTORY AND HYSTERICS

Not at all certain he understood what Daphne's motive was, John left her at the elevator and went in search of intel. That's what Daphne called it.

"We need more information about this hotel, love," she'd said. "Think of it as gathering intel."

"What kind of information? The size of the estate and when it was built kind?"

"Probably more the 'is this place for sale?' kind. Better yet, are the staff all happy?"

Shaking his head, he kissed her cheek. What on earth did she mean? How could he find answers with her vague instructions?

On the wall not far from the reception desk was a large photograph of the hotel taken from the front with a dozen or so people in hotel uniforms posing on the driveway. As good a place as any to begin. Although the photograph was in sepia tones, the faces of some of the staff gave away how recent it was. He recognised Col straight away, who had his arm around the shoulders of a woman about the same age. She was broad shouldered with cropped hair and although he'd only caught a glimpse of one person of that description, he knew it was Cherry, who he'd seen in one of the 4WDs.

Mandy was at the end of a row but wore a white blouse and skirt, not her manager's uniform.

"I was the office girl."

John hadn't heard Mandy approach.

"And now you manage the retreat?"

She smiled. There were lines of exhaustion around her eyes. Daphne had said Mandy was up most of the previous night and he'd seen her every time he'd been in the foyer, so when did she sleep?

"The owners—that's Mr and Mrs Burton in the middle of the front row—had the right idea about developing this property but they weren't hoteliers. After two years they wanted to go back to travelling and promoted me rather than hire a new manager. I was already handling most of the administration and was studying to get my degree in business management."

"And you live here all the time?"

"All of it. Haven't had a real break in almost three years but for the most part I love what I do."

"Not so much when there are strange happenings such as this evening's?"

She laughed shortly. "The last couple of days have had their moments."

What is Daphne trying to figure out? She said about staff being happy.

"From my perspective, as a first-time guest who is planning to return, you run the place beautifully. I imagine you have a tight-knit team behind you."

The smile she'd had since coming to talk with him faded. "Hearthstone has good staff. Maisie is awesome and does a lot more than run the day spa. We have two chefs here and I can't imagine working without them. Housekeeping is brilliant, and so on. So, yes. A good team."

He gestured to the photo. "Col and Cherry? Apart from collecting guests from the carpark, what is their role?"

"Whatever they want, lately." She put her hand over her mouth, eyes wide. "I am so sorry." Her words were muffled until she dropped her hand. "I wouldn't ever normally say something without thinking so please accept my apology."

"Honesty is a good thing and I'm not on anyone's side apart from the truth so say what you feel. Daphne and I worked together in close quarters for decades and the times we had other realtors or assistants working for us, they'd always say how united a team we were."

"Oh, you are! I've watched you together and can only hope to have such a loving relationship myself one day."

This warmed his heart. And made him proud of his wife.

"Very kind of you to say." He tapped the photo right where Col stood. "I imagine having a married couple working for you has its challenges. Sometimes couples fight when they work together."

Bait the hook.

Mandy glanced around. There was nobody at all in the foyer except the two of them and she nodded as though she had just had a debate with herself and made a decision.

"Col and Cherry were here for a year before me. Col used to work for a big hotel chain and managed an island resort for a while. Cherry was in the army when they met and knows her way around any vehicle. Any machine. Anyway, they were here when I was hired to fix a few issues on the administration side of things. Mr Burton had made a bit of a mess." She laughed with real humour this time. "To say the least! Col was the concierge. I know, hard to imagine, but he was good at it. And he wanted the job which I was given."

Mandy bit her lip and scanned the room again, her eyes widening as they stopped on the front door. John followed her stare. Col was speaking to the staff member stationed out there. He waved his arms around and the other person, a young man, stepped back.

"Does he do that often?"

"Too often. Don't get me wrong. He isn't a bad person. And when I was given the promotion, he and Cherry were fantastic and helped me. But lately…"

"Lately?"

She shrugged. "They aren't happy here anymore. I'd better see how the police officers' uniforms are going. Thank goodness for our lovely housekeeping staff who are so flexible with their hours. Like all of us this weekend."

As Mandy walked away, her head down, he wanted to say something. Find a way to reassure her that she was doing an incredible job under trying circumstances. She glanced at him over her shoulder.

"Hey. Thanks for listening."

Col pushed the front door open and spent a minute brushing rain from his hair. His shirt was soaked through and there was water on the floor around him.

"Long day?" Might as well see what Col could add to John's growing collection of information. Intel.

With a scowl, Col kicked off one boot then the other and carried them over, his socks leaving wet prints on the timber. "Mate, you have no idea. And now it's bucketing down again so I can't even do my job without getting drenched for what, the fourth or fifth time today?"

"At least Stacy was found safe."

"Yeah. Stupid woman trying to get down the mountain on foot. Through the bush no less. She's been a pain every time she comes here."

"Every time?"

Col stared at him. "Sorry. She a friend?"

"Goodness, no. Only met her tonight. Wet and bedraggled."

"Yeah. Well, she's trouble. Speaking out of turn here but I have no idea why a decent association like Audrey's would employ such a loser. This isn't the first night I've spent out looking for her instead of cuddling up to my wife. But at least her behaviour has caught up with her and she's going to end up going away for a long time."

The glee on Col's face was disconcerting. Glee. And something else.

"You don't seem surprised," John said.

With a shrug, Col glanced at the photo on the wall. "Some people just deserve what they get. Might take a while but it comes. And now I'm going to get into dry clothes. Goodnight."

"Goodnight."

John worked out the second emotion on Col's face. It was hatred.

Even if Daphne had not known which room was Stacy's, the continuing sobs would have given her a decent clue. A couple of other doors in the hallway were open a few inches as people peeked out.

The door to the suite was open and the wheelchair was stationary in the living room. Stacy had a box of tissues on her lap and held a fistful. Both police officers searched the living room, wearing gloves and taking care to replace anything they moved, although there was a growing pile on one chair as the clothes on the floor were inspected. It was the neatest and most ordered search Daphne could imagine.

"I really do need to use the bathroom." Stacy began to get out of the wheelchair and Leon turned around.

"We need to go in there and search before you do."

Stacy's face couldn't get much redder.

"What if you two go there first and I'll stay with Stacy?" Daphne wasn't about to leave the other woman desperate for a bathroom stop. "Either that, or I can take her to my suite and let her use my bathroom?"

"Oh, Daphne, thank you. They won't listen to me."

"We are listening. We just need to do our job." This was Constable Patterson. "And you can't take the suspect anywhere."

"Suspect! But I'm—"

Daphne put a hand on Stacy's shoulder. "Officers, Stacy is a person first and foremost and requires access to a bathroom. I'm going to wheel her to my suite to use mine and then return her. No deviations and apart from the couple of minutes with a closed bathroom door between us, she won't be out of my sight."

The constables exchanged a glance. "Five minutes, Mrs Jones. Miss Chester? No disappearing."

"I promise. I can barely use my ankle anyway."

"Just say thank you," Daphne whispered as she took the handles.

"Thank you."

A moment later they were zooming along the hallway as fast as Daphne could manage. "Hold on, dear. Only a couple of minutes."

"You are so kind, Daphne. From the first time we met you've been so sweet and nice to me. And understanding. I really, really appreciate you standing up for me."

I'm taking you to a bathroom. Nothing else.

"You need a chance to wash your face and take a breath," Daphne said.

"I need a few more glasses of wine!"

"Are you up to telling me why you were leaving the retreat on foot, at night? We were all so worried."

"Um. I went for a walk to clear my head. The stuff people were saying at the dinner really upset me. Pointing fingers at me. Everyone seems nice but there's a lot of jealousy because I'm paid and I have access to Rupert all the time."

"Rupert? As president, isn't he available to members if they need him?"

"Not the way I was." She blew her nose as Daphne powered through the lounge area. "We've worked closely to optimise the benefits to the members. I did most of my work from my home office, but we met up weekly to go over things. Usually at his houseboat. Not that I like being on the water, but I did like his cats."

"And your relationship with Rupert... Oh, I really don't mean to pry..."

I really do mean to.

"You can ask me anything. We are close friends. Nothing more. And even though he, well, he got upset with me and let Audrey say those nasty things? There never was any issue. Not ever."

"It did surprise me."

"He's in shock. Darren was his friend for something like twenty years so of course he's distressed. We both are." Another sob.

Enough already. "Almost there!"

With a turn of the key, Daphne had the door open and Stacy took over, using the hand rims on the wheels to get to the door of the bedroom.

"The bathroom is through here." She helped Stacy up and between the two of them, they got her to the bathroom. "Okay on your own?"

"I'll hop."

After closing the door, Daphne went to the French doors. Outside, the rain had eased. She'd have liked to open the doors and let some of the warmish night air into the room, but it would have to wait. The bed called to her. Inviting her to climb into the sheets and close her eyes for a while. What a mess this day had been. The last twenty-four hours for that matter. Surely nothing else could go wrong before bedtime?

"Oh no!"

The bathroom door opened and Stacy, who looked much fresher, grinned. "The window is too small to climb out."

Daphne had to laugh and Stacy joined in. But the younger woman's laughter turned back into tears and by the time she flopped into the wheelchair, her cheeks were wet again.

"Here's another box of tissues, dear. You are exhausted and hurt and have had a loss so no wonder you are emotional."

"Why is this happening, Daphne?" Stacy cried. "I would never harm Rupert. Nor anyone."

"Let's get you back to your room before those gentlemen come looking." Daphne pushed the wheelchair out of the suite and locked the door before walking at a much slower pace than the trip over. "You don't tell me what made you try to leave the estate?"

"I heard Col and his team." Stacy blew her nose, getting herself back under control. "They had flashlights and were joking about finding me and throwing me in the fountain to teach me a lesson. Gave me a scare and I took off. Next thing I knew, the ground slipped beneath my feet and I was rolling down a steep embankment."

"I'm so sorry. What a horrible thing for them to say. And earlier you said something else about Col. About not trusting someone with a vested interest? What was that about?"

There was no reply. Just sniffles.

They were almost back at Stacy's room and without doubt, the police would have discovered the magnets for themselves. Whatever happened next, probably there'd be no further chance to ask questions and the opportunity to put the pieces together might be lost. This was about more than the accusations thrown at Stacy. Much more.

"Please, Stacy? I'm on your side."

Stacy looked over her shoulder, her eyes puffy. "Why?"

"I like to find out the truth. And I'm not convinced the police have all the relevant information yet. You need to talk to them about what you know or suspect."

"Col and Cherry? They are involved with—"

"There you are." Constable Patterson came around the last corner. "We need you back in your room please, Miss Chester."

The opportunity to find out who Col and Cherry were involved with was gone as the police officer took the wheelchair from Daphne. Before she could say anything, all three of them were back in Stacy's room.

"In here, please." Leon was in the bedroom.

The suitcase was open on the bed.

"Miss Chester. We have located a number of items in this room which we believe are connected to a possible attempt on the life of Rupert Witherspoon. Once the road is clear you'll accompany us to the local station for further questioning and a team will arrive to process this room."

"Are you... are you arresting me?"

From the grim look on Leon's face that was exactly what they were going to do.

TWENTY-FOUR
DONE. NOT DUSTED

"Do you mind if I cancel the massages?"

They sat on the balcony where Daphne was nursing a cold cup of coffee. Well, it must be getting cold because she hadn't sipped it in ten minutes or so. John had offered to get a fresh one, but she'd just given him a tired smile and said this one was fine.

They'd got back to the suite closer to one than midnight and fallen into bed. He'd have let her sleep in for as long as she needed, but the minute he stirred, so did she.

"Of course, we can cancel. But there's no hurry for us to leave. Mandy said to take our time so I can see if the day spa can push the appointment back a bit." John reached over and rubbed one of her shoulders. "Wouldn't a massage feel good?"

"Maybe. I'll wait a few more minutes before deciding." Her hand found his and squeezed it. "I don't remember feeling so tired and so... flat."

"Last night was hard going. But you can't blame yourself for what happened to Stacy."

"If I hadn't shown those photos to the police. Or given them the notes."

She'd handed those to Leon while the other officer was speaking with Stacy.

He shuffled his seat close, and put an arm around her and she leaned her head on his shoulder with a sigh.

"What choice did you have, Daph? Keep potentially vital information to yourself and risk getting in trouble with the law? Or even worse, let her get away with her plan to harm Rupert?"

"I know. But something isn't sitting right, and I'm not convinced she hasn't been set up. I'm struggling to put the pieces together, though, and I fear time will run out."

There was a tap on the door and John kissed the top of Daphne's head as he stood. "Be right back."

It was room service.

"Don't think this is for us."

"It was ordered on your behalf, sir."

Not wishing to argue, John thanked the young woman who'd wheeled the small cart up and took it through to the balcony.

"Did you happen to order breakfast?"

"I did."

Rupert stood at his balcony, in his dressing gown. His hair was a mess, and he looked even more exhausted than Daphne. But his smile was kind.

"You two were in the thick of things last night and I woke up starving and couldn't bear thinking you both might be as well. There's a selection so I hope it helps."

Daphne blinked rapidly.

Don't cry, doll.

Rupert put both hands on the balustrade and leaned toward them. "Listen, buttercup. It is breakfast not a wake so no waterworks."

She burst into laughter.

"Better. Now, eat up and when you are ready can the three of us sit down and have a talk about what's happened? Just text me."

"Thank you, Rupert. This was thoughtful of you," John said.

The other man waved and went back inside.

"Remind me to tell him no more calling me buttercup,"

Daphne said as she lifted the lid off a plate. "After we eat this, of course."

"He is very generous. I think he respects you a lot, doll."

"Goes both ways. Oh, are those pancakes under there?"

After what proved to be a delicious and much-needed breakfast, John and Daphne made their way to the roof. Rupert waited at one of the tables, scrolling on his phone until he noticed them approach. He got to his feet, offering his hand to John to shake.

"Thank you both. Please, take a seat. I took the liberty of ordering coffee which will be here shortly."

Rupert wore jeans and a striped shirt, his hair back in its ponytail and sunglasses pushed up on the top of his head. It was a good look on him. Not that John had enough hair left to grow it long even if he was brave enough to change the style of decades.

"When do you leave?" Rupert asked.

"The original plan was about eleven. Mandy said we can check out later if we want to," Daphne said. "I'm rather keen to get back to Bluebell and..."

"Go? Leave behind this crazy place you got dragged into?" Rupert nodded to himself. "I feel the same. Except I'm heading back to reporters and chaos."

"Because of Stacy?" John asked.

"Because of Darren."

Coffee arrived and they waited until the server left before resuming the conversation. It was Daphne who had questions and for the first time since they'd returned to their room last night, John saw a glimmer of real interest in her eyes.

"I know Darren is... sorry, was, a member of the association, but why should his car accident put you in that position?" she asked.

He seemed to think about the question, stirring his coffee for a while.

Daphne pressed on. "It *was* an accident?"

Rupert raised his eyes to look at her. "I don't know."

Something changed with Daphne. She straightened and her chin lifted. "So, you believe somebody else was responsible."

"Stacy had no way to cause his car to crash into the river. I've considered every possibility and keep coming up with nothing of any use. Which is why I wanted us to talk. Before the police have further questions."

I have questions.

"My understanding is that Stacy is charged with some kind of intent to harm you, Rupert. Not Darren. Are you of the opinion that she would hurt both of you?" John asked.

"Oh. Great question, love."

"So, here's the thing." Rupert gazed at John, then Daphne. "Stacy isn't the person the police think. She has her issues... don't we all? But she loves this association with a passion, and I can't see her doing anything to damage it. Her job means the world to her and for several years she was the most wonderful person to have on board."

"Until?" Daphne leaned her elbows on the table with the cup aloft between her hands.

"Until she mistook our friendship for something more. My fault. Like Darren, I'm a little flamboyant if you hadn't noticed." He grinned. "Part of my success as a celebrant, since I attract couples who enjoy my flair and humour."

"Last night Audrey said Stacy had needed to be told to back off... well, something like that. And you mentioned thinking you'd both moved past some unpleasantness. How bad was it, Rupert?"

"Audrey exaggerated everything. And I was in shock when I heard about the magnets. I'm paranoid about interfering with the pacemaker because, quite frankly, I don't wish to die. Particularly not from something preventable. Stacy was carrying on and all I could think about was poor Darren in the river and her having magnets, one of which ended up in my jacket." He picked up his coffee and drank.

Inside the restaurant, a few tables were occupied but out here, they were the only ones. It made for a private place to talk.

Rupert put his cup down. "Stacy and I had a very quiet and frank chat about keeping our relationship professional. It wasn't broadcasted yet somehow, Audrey found out. The only person I'd said a word to was Darren so you can make up your own mind on that."

"Do you think Stacy held a grudge against Darren for telling his wife?"

"Not in the least. She adored him. And somehow it turned her attention from me to him. And it was right before last year's conference and he did himself, or Stacy, no favours by going out searching for the laptop with her."

Daphne made an odd sound. She turned it into clearing her throat and then busied herself sipping coffee. Something had clicked. Something she didn't want to mention in front of Rupert.

Rupert's phone buzzed. "Audrey is looking for me. Now the road is clear she wants to get down the mountain." He pushed himself to his feet. "I'll see you both before you leave?"

"We'll be here for a while yet," Daphne said.

With his customary wave, Rupert left with the walk of a tired man.

"Did you just say we'll be here for a while?"

"I did. We have a murder to solve."

TWENTY-FIVE
CLUTCHING AT CLUES

The minute Rupert said the word 'laptop' a whole lot of pieces fell into place. For a minute she mentally kicked herself for overlooking the obvious and forgetting important facts, but she pushed that aside. She needed a clear head now.

"We need to go back to our suite, love."

She wasn't waiting around for another minute. John caught up with her at the top of the stairs. "I knew you'd worked something out back there."

"When I kind of gurgled?"

"You covered it well enough to fool Rupert. But not me."

"You know me far too well."

As they reached the lounge area on their floor, Leon came around the corner pushing the wheelchair with Stacy in it. The last Daphne had heard, she'd been given another room for the night and the officers would share shifts outside her door, not that she'd have got far even if she did intend to disappear.

"Daphne! Please don't let them take me." Stacy grabbed her hand as Leon stopped and pushed the down button on the elevator. "I didn't do anything wrong."

There were no more tears. Stacy's skin was paler than normal and her eyes had dark shadows beneath them. Her foot was newly bandaged and she carried her handbag on her lap.

"And you'll be able to get some legal help, dear. The best way to prove your innocence is to be completely honest and as helpful as possible. Now isn't the time to hide anything."

Leon offered a grateful smile as the doors opened. "We have one of the hotel shuttles waiting."

"Oh. Just so you know, I think Audrey is also waiting for one."

"No, no! I can't be in the same one. Please, Leon? Please don't make me?" Stacy beseeched.

"Mrs Sutton will have to wait for the next one. We need to get you to our patrol car and to the station." Leon pushed the wheelchair into the elevator and turned it. "No sharing rides."

As the doors closed, Stacy was smiling widely at the police officer. "You are so kind to me..."

When they reached their suite, they were both still grinning at Stacy's turnaround.

"Wonder if she's found older men too trying," John said, holding the door open for Daphne. "Better luck with a younger one."

"Particularly one who she perceives might help her."

First point of call was finding her latest notebook and second was sitting on the balcony with it. John got them both a glass of water and then brought his laptop out. "I want to download those photos I took the other day."

"Good idea, love. I remembered something this morning. About a laptop."

How she'd forgotten was beyond her. Probably being almost caught by Audrey had something to do with it.

"What laptop?" John had his open, but his attention was on her.

"Quick version. Audrey did a session which turned out to be more self-promotion than anything."

"For her bridal shops?"

"More for her new wedding hub. The committee gave her

permission to showcase it with an offer for association members, but she struggled a bit when people asked hard questions and made a comment about wishing she had the presentation which was on a laptop. And the laptop was with Darren, who was supposed to bring it with him."

Opening the notebook, she quickly wrote 'where is the laptop?'.

"Should we be letting the police know to look out for his laptop in the car?" John asked. "Except, what makes it important now?"

Am I completely off base?

"There's a chance—a very small chance—that the laptop is here. In the hotel."

"And dare I ask why you believe this?"

"Because I saw one where it shouldn't have been."

The expression of defeat on John's face almost made her laugh aloud. Not because it was funny but because it was predictable. He was getting used to this newfound sleuthing of hers and offered less resistance each time.

"I saw it when I was in Darren's room. The one he was meant to have."

"Daphne Jones."

"Sorry. But you knew I was in there. With everything else going on, I had forgotten about the laptop until Rupert mentioned the word and then it came back to me. But I'm probably wrong because I only saw a laptop bag. I didn't look inside it," she said.

"I guess I should be proud of you for restraining yourself."

She giggled and began to list her other observations. John plugged his phone into his laptop to move the photos then began going through them. It was pleasant to sit here in the morning air. Not too warm, and shaded until the sun moved around the hotel. Her shoulders untensed a bit as she wrote, reminding her about the day spa. In case Maisie was busy with someone, she sent a quick text message, asking if it was possible to change the time until later in the day.

In seconds there was an affirmative response with a new time.

"Maisie has let me change our appointment to midday."

"Mm-hm."

Something had John's interest. Daphne peered around at his screen which was zoomed in on... water? He zoomed out. It was the fountain.

"What were you looking at in there?"

"Not sure. I think there might be a translucent item about the size of a pebble. Probably nothing but a bit of rubbish dropped in by a bird or the wind."

He zoomed in as close as he could but lost clarity.

"There's the barest outline there."

From below the balcony, voices rose and they both looked down. Stacy was in the back seat of one of the hotel's 4WDs, the door closed but window open. Cherry stood near the back watching on while Audrey complained to Leon. Only bits of the conversation were audible, but it was obvious she was cross about being relegated to the next lift down.

"Can you see the other officer?" she asked.

"I imagine he's staying here until the forensics people arrive."

Audrey stomped away from Leon, who climbed in beside Stacy. Cherry followed Audrey, putting a hand on her shoulder, and walking with her for a few feet, their heads close together as they talked.

"They look cosy. I wonder what's being said." Daphne added their names to her list with question marks beside them. "Don't think I've spoken to Cherry at all. I know Col thinks well of Audrey and badly of Stacy."

"That's true. Last night he said Stacy was getting what was coming to her. Said she'd been a pain more than once and he was surprised an association... let me think what he said... ah, an associ-ation like Audrey's would employ someone like Stacy."

"Like Audrey's? As though she ran it."

John nodded. "We haven't had a proper chance for me to tell you what I found out last night. Not that it was a lot."

Closing her notebook, she gave him her full attention as he told her about the framed photograph where he and Mandy had spoken about the background of the hotel, its owners, and some of the dynamics of the staff. How she'd excused herself when Col came back inside. And Col's enjoyment of Stacy's situation.

Bit by bit, the pieces fell into place.

"John? Are you up for a short walk?"

It was a short walk. In search of Constable Patterson, they went to Stacy's room which was locked with a 'do not disturb' sign on.

"Either he's having a nap or it's to keep housekeeping out," Daphne said. "Reception it is."

Guests were checking out and a line of 4WDs waited outside. Staff ferried luggage out and there was an air of urgency in the area around reception. Three staff worked to process the guests and there were lots of 'goodbyes' and 'see you next time' as people left.

There was no sign of the police officer, nor Mandy. But Col was talking to Audrey just inside the door. They stood close together.

"Daph, look over near the front door," he said quietly. "Tell me there's more than a casual connection between Audrey, Cherry, and Col."

"You're right. There's more to it. I remember Audrey telling Rupert she didn't like the way some of the front desk staff treated her. That was on the first night. I wonder if she means Mandy."

Gloria and Ted finished at the front of the line and came across to say goodbye, with kisses from her and handshakes from him.

"What a shame this weekend had so many unpleasant moments, Daphne. I hope it hasn't put you off our association. We always cover the hotel cost of the recipient of the outstanding client satisfaction award but have never expected to get back so much from one. You caught a killer." Gloria held both of Daphne's hands. "I've enjoyed my time with you very much."

"Not put me off at all. And I feel the same about you."

"Well, I think we need to wait out the front for a driver, so see you both again." Ted took Gloria's arm and they wound their way through the line.

"Lovely people." John liked Ted and had already arranged a meet-up to fish early next year.

"Look."

Mandy headed toward Col and Audrey. She must have been outside, and she squinted as she scanned the foyer as John had seen her do more than once. When she reached them, she said something to Audrey then to Col, who folded his arms. Mandy lifted her chin and spoke again and this time he smirked and stalked across to meet Gloria and Ted. When Mandy turned to leave, Audrey grabbed her arm and snapped something at her.

"I know we can't hear from this distance, but do you think we need to rescue Mandy? Audrey is furious."

"Let's try."

Before they were halfway there, Mandy shook herself loose and left Audrey in mid-sentence. Or mid-screech.

"So, start looking for a new job."

They made a beeline for Mandy, who held herself stiffly as if she half expected Audrey to throw something at her. Something more than angry words.

"Are you okay, dear?"

"Um. Yes. Sorry, did you need me?"

"We think you need to stay away from that particular guest. She really isn't very nice, is she?" Daphne said.

Mandy's lips flicked up for a second. "Best I don't answer."

"We get the feeling Mrs Sutton is very friendly with Col and Cherry."

"Quite honestly, yes. It probably doesn't matter what I say anymore because my job here will only last until she finalises her purchase of Hearthstone. The day it happens, I'll be fired and those two will take over." Mandy's eyes glistened. "I love my job, and I'll keep doing it the best I can until that happens. Please excuse me." Head down, she disappeared into the office behind the reception desk.

Audrey glared at them across the room. For just a second, John considered asking her why she had a problem with Mandy, let alone with his wife. But the second passed and instead, he found Daphne's hand.

"I think a touch of sunshine is in order."

TWENTY-SIX

SPARKLY THINGS

"Of all the nerve!"

Daphne had managed to control her outrage until they walked out of earshot of the guests and staff outside the hotel. Every few minutes a 4WD, packed with guests and luggage, drove off. They'd passed Audrey as they'd left the foyer, but it was only John's firm grip of her hand which stopped her having words with the other woman.

"Calm down."

"How dare she tell Mandy, who is so sweet and so capable, to look for a new job. She doesn't own the hotel yet."

"Perhaps she never will."

"Well, I'd like to see her face if she can't buy it. But why wouldn't she be able to?"

They slowed down as the path inclined.

"Expensive things, hotels. Didn't you tell me Darren was going to have to cash in his shares to help finance it?"

She stopped dead. "Audrey needed his money for her project. He was on the fence about it. But what if he'd told her no? What if her desire to buy this place outweighed her love for her husband?"

"I'm not sure I follow where you're heading. The police seem pretty sure Stacy made up the story about seeing a body and it's been pointed out more than once that Darren never arrived. What does Audrey and Darren have to do with Stacy?" John said.

Every time she thought she'd worked this out, logic said otherwise.

"Mrs Jones? Mr Jones?"

Constable Patterson ran toward them from the hotel. He was back in his uniform and carried a phone. When he reached them, he was puffing.

"Everything alright, constable?" John asked.

"Pat. Please, Pat is good."

Pat Patterson? Or Pat short for Patterson? And why are names so interesting?

He continued, "Do you mind if we have a word?"

"Actually, we had been looking for you earlier, but needed to check something," Daphne said.

"What did you need me for?"

"I may have some helpful information. Or it may not be. But why were you chasing us down?"

"I got a call from Leon. Constable Finnegan. He's arrived at the station and was given an update on Darren Sutton. A rather strange one. A witness came forward to say they'd seen a car matching the description of Mr Sutton's parked between trees not far from where it entered the water. The spot in question is a bushy area between the road and river. Only a few metres wide but pretty dense."

Hidden on purpose?

"It was in the morning, many hours before the car was found in the river. The witness was jogging and checked the car, worried someone might be unwell. It was empty, apart from a suitcase in the back seat," Pat said. "He forgot about it until news got around town. Sometime between then and when it was found, the car came off the road a hundred or so metres further along, where there's a hill sloping down to the water. No signs of tyre marks. Nothing to indicate braking. And the car was in neutral."

Daphne's heart sped up. There was a tingle in her stomach and the hairs on the back of her arms stood up. This was where it would all come together. The clues. The hints. The speculation. The answers were so close she could almost see them.

John frowned. "Darren's car parked but no Darren, then a few hours later, he's in the car and deceased in the river. How does that work?"

"It doesn't," Pat said.

"He died on Friday night and his body wasn't found until Saturday night. Is that what you are saying?" John asked.

"It is. There is a preliminary time of death as being the early hours of Saturday morning."

"How early?" Daphne almost held her breath.

"Don't know. Before dawn, though, because of certain indicators. But I'm not the person to ask. And the reason I chased after you both is to ask you, Mrs Jones, if you remembered seeing anything else in or around the fountain."

She glanced at John. What if she had this all wrong? He gave her an encouraging smile and her doubt evaporated.

"Pat? I can only give you my observations and they might help, or hinder, but if you want them, can we keep going? We are heading to the perfect place to discuss this."

"Sorry? Where?"

"The fountain on top of a mountain."

"Do you remember anything more about being out here the other night?" Pat walked around the fountain slowly, gazing into the water.

Still no cascading waterfall. The water barely moved.

"Only what I already told you and Leon earlier, after you searched Stacy's room. My first impression was of something, someone, beneath Rupert's jacket. I thought it was him."

"What changed your mind, Mrs Jones?"

"Please, just call me Daphne. I much prefer it." She smiled at the young officer. Having lived her life in small towns, she had little time for formality, certainly about herself. She was Daphne, or Daph, to everyone who knew her.

"Why didn't you check beneath the jacket?" he asked.

"I've asked myself that over and over. Had I done so, then Stacy might not be in the mess she is."

Pat stopped his visual exploration of the bottom of the fountain and looked at her. "There was a fair amount of physical evidence pointing to her having placed a magnet or magnets into Mr Witherspoon's jacket. The notes you provided showed her intent to lure him here. And she has now admitted she wrote both of them."

John cleared his throat. "Only one. The second note is an apology for getting his room number wrong."

"Covering her tracks. Allegedly." Pat shrugged. "You went for help and brought Rupert back. Earlier, you mentioned he'd been shocked to find his jacket here."

"Annoyed, I think was my word. He has several expensive jackets and thought it was ruined by being in the water. When he and I arrived here, we were alone. No sign of Stacy. He pulled his jacket out and laid it on the grass. She ran over from the corner." She pointed. "For some reason she was convinced the body was taken in that direction."

Pat tapped on his phone. "Terrible coverage. Ah... there we go." He showed them a map of the property, pinching the screen to find the English garden. "Okay. This is interesting." He glanced toward the corner. "If I'm reading this right, about ten metres from the corner there is a track wide enough for a vehicle. It links back to the main driveway..." He moved the map on the screen. "Here. Hm." It was within sight of the hotel.

Her stomach lurched and she reached out a hand to John.

"Daph?"

"I think I know what happened. Or some of it. I should never have left poor Stacy on her own."

"Would you like to sit?"

"No, thank you. I'd like for us to find something. In the bottom of the fountain." She pointed to the water. "I'd like for us to locate a diamond."

He had the world's smartest sleuth as his wife and he couldn't be prouder.

For long minutes, John and Pat stared at the water searching for the tell-tale glint from the photo of the object on his phone. While they did that, Daphne disappeared with a cryptic comment about fishing.

"Does she do this often?" Pat had his hands in the water, gently feeling along the bottom.

"Find connections?"

Pat laughed. "I was going to say does she play amateur sleuth often? But that will do."

"Yes to both. She has a knack of seeing the big picture and then the fine details. Like being really good at jigsaw puzzles."

"Is she?"

"Nope. She's terrible at them."

They both laughed.

The water was cool on John's hands as the sun rose above them. Soon it would be uncomfortably warm and with the rise in humidity, no doubt another storm would brew later today. When it did, he would have Daphne and Bluebell far away from here. She had no commitments for a fortnight, and it was about time they went home, at least for a few days. Let her sit on the beach in Rivers End and catch up with their friends.

"Have you found it yet?" Daphne puffed a bit. She must have walked fast to get to the hotel and back in such a short time.

"What have you got there?" Pat asked.

"Never been fishing, young man?" John grinned.

Daphne had one of his fishing nets. The smallest one with the tightest mesh.

Clever, clever cookie.

He kissed her cheek. "Perfect."

"Well, thank you. But I haven't even straightened my hair yet!"

They both laughed as Pat joined them.

"Ready to go diamond fishing?" John asked him.

While the men played with the net in the fountain, Daphne sat on the stone bench from the first day, running through every second of that night in her head.

What had she forgotten?

When she'd walked here looking for Stacy, she'd felt someone watching her. But who? And had that person followed her to the garden?

Or were they a lookout?

Had other people been here when she'd arrived? Hidden against the long and dark hedges, or behind statues? A shiver went down her spine. Stacy might have been in terrible danger if she'd accidentally stumbled upon a fresh murder.

So might you.

It didn't bear considering.

Then there was the matter of the water.

Daphne returned to the fountain. "Any luck yet?"

"Not yet." Pat concentrated on the water as John moved the net along the bottom.

"John has super sharp eyes. Maybe if you change over for a bit?"

"Fair enough." Pat didn't seem offended as he took the net from John.

"How deep do you think the water is?" she asked.

"About a foot. Eighteen inches max. Why's that?" John answered as he watched the slow and steady motion of the net.

She mentally gauged the depth of a human male's torso lying down.

"Deep enough for a normal sized body to be mostly submerged, I imagine. And if a jacket was over them, it would float, or at least, the arms would."

"If you are asking if a body could have been in the fountain and covered by this level of water, then I believe it could," Pat said. "Whether it was is another thing."

"I remember Rupert standing in the fountain to retrieve his jacket. The water almost touched the hem of his dressing gown, and he is fairly tall. Actually..." She retraced her steps of the other night, going around the fountain flashing the light from her phone into the water searching for the body. "Oh. I'd forgotten."

Both men glanced up.

"I just remembered when Rupert and I were here I found a strip of the bricks which were soaking wet. It was on this side, facing that corner. I think that is why Stacy went there looking because when she couldn't catch up with me to ask me to look for her glasses, she came back here, only to find the body missing. She either saw someone disappearing into the corner, or figured the body was carried away in the same direction."

"Pat... a bit more to your left. Slowly." John's face was as close to the water as it could be without touching it. "Stop for a sec." His hand snaked to the bottom, and he gently moved it back and forth. "Now!"

With a sudden flick of the net, Pat scooped fast, lifting the net from the water in one movement.

"Did you get it?" Daphne couldn't see as Pat and John worked together to extricate what they'd found. If she was right...

"Ah. Look at this."

On the palm of his hand, John held a small, multi-faceted diamond. Under the sun it sparkled as droplets of water slid off its surface.

"You are both amazing."

Pat opened a small zip-lock bag. "It looks like a diamond, not that I'm any kind of expert, but I don't understand the significance. Is it from a ring?"

"Not a ring. But we're going to have to move fast now." To prove her point, Daphne was already on her way. "We have to stop her leaving with the evidence."

TWENTY-SEVEN

WHEN DIAMONDS AREN'T
A GIRL'S BEST FRIEND

Daphne was near the tennis courts by the time they caught up with her. Shoving damp feet into shoes wasn't easy and both men then had to jog.

"Do you know who she means?" Pat puffed.

"Audrey is my guess."

John glanced at his watch. Audrey had wanted Cherry to drive her down the mountain, but Cherry had taken Leon and Stacy instead. Col was tied up with Gloria and Ted which meant unless Audrey accepted another driver, she'd wait for Cherry to return.

Daphne slowed to let them catch her. "It will depend on how important it is for her to go with Cherry. Or whether she has any inkling we're onto her."

"Wait a second. I mean, can we stop for a minute to talk please?" Pat looked so confused that Daphne nodded and they came to a halt.

From here, the hotel was in view. A 4WD appeared from the direction of the exit.

"Why do I need to stop Audrey leaving?" Pat asked. He checked his phone and grimaced as if seeing no coverage again.

"I can't explain it all. But I think you need to check her luggage for two things. One is an earring, missing a diamond. It went missing between her wearing it to dinner on Friday night and morning tea Saturday. The other item is a laptop computer which according to Audrey, didn't arrive here for a presentation she made because her husband was bringing it with him."

Pat scratched his chin. "Unless I have due cause to search her luggage, I can't touch it. Nor can I stop her leaving."

Daphne's shoulders slumped. "Then she's about to get away with murder."

"Who did she murder, Mrs... sorry, Daphne?"

"Well, her husband, of course. Or she helped. But she is certainly behind it."

The 4WD stopped at the front of the hotel and Cherry climbed out and headed into the hotel.

"Constable Patterson, at least ask some questions. Ask if the laptop seen in her husband's room is hers. If she's innocent, why would she object to helping?"

He hesitated.

John started walking and Daphne quickly joined him. "Come on, Pat. You can probably ask the hotel not to transport her. At least not until you have a chance to ask some questions."

"Thank you, love," Daphne whispered.

"I have an idea. And I'm hoping Mandy might assist us."

Daphne had all the clues. Probably all the answers. Oh, please, let there be enough time to persuade the police before it was too late.

John excused himself at the hotel entrance and hurried inside.

There were no other 4WDs around and the foyer looked deserted through the open doors so the guests must have all been transported. Pat, with Daphne right behind him, went straight to the back of the parked vehicle, its door open. It was empty and spotless.

"I wonder if they are always so clean," he said.

"Cherry claimed a guest was carsick and she took the vehicle to town to clean it. But she'd do that if there'd been a wet body in it. I imagine."

Pat shot a look at Daphne and she smiled.

"I'm beginning to see where you are going with this," he said. "This is the same vehicle which got caught in town with the storm?"

"It is. I remember the licence plate. All of them are personalised as HHCR for Hearthstone High Country Retreat, then a number. I saw her drive HHCR03 down the driveway early on Saturday morning."

His phone dinged and he grabbed it out. "Thank goodness. Give me a minute, please."

He dialled and walked a few paces away to speak.

Another 4WD nosed along the driveway. And Audrey was coming her way.

"How sweet. Here to say goodbye?" Audrey oozed confidence and her smile was sickly sweet. "Most of the others left and I'd have thought you'd be with them."

"Not just yet. There's some business to finish first."

Audrey snorted. "What kind of business? Think you've uncovered a crime?"

There was no way Daphne was answering that. She ran her fingers across her lips in a zipping motion. Audrey rolled her eyes and turned her back.

The second 4WD pulled up with Col behind the wheel. He nodded to Audrey and glanced at Daphne before heading into the hotel. A minute later he emerged with some luggage and Cherry behind him, carrying more.

Up close, Cherry was powerfully built. Muscular arms and legs beneath shorts and shirt. She certainly had no issue with the luggage. She gave Daphne an odd look but not so much as a smile or hello.

"Can we get a move on, guys?" Audrey opened the front passenger door and put her handbag in the footwell. "I have so many people to talk to about Darren."

"Mrs Sutton, before you leave, I have a couple of quick questions. If you don't mind?" Pat was back.

"Well, I do mind. Your partner prevented me from leaving earlier and I'm not about to be delayed again. I have a funeral to arrange."

"And I am sorry for your loss. This won't take long."

Cherry slammed the back door and came around to the side. "Hop in. I'll get you back to your car." She put her hand on the door and stared at Pat.

"Cherry? Wait on please." Mandy, with John at her side, hurried to the side of the vehicle.

"What now?" Audrey snarled. "Somebody needs to find Rupert. I want him to see what nonsense you're pulling this time."

Cherry grinned.

"This vehicle is unavailable, sorry. I'll have the keys, thank you." Mandy held out her hand.

"Now listen here—" Cherry began.

"Unavailable, why?" Col demanded.

"I have a valid reason."

"Bull. Come on. We'll take the other car." Col opened the back door as if to get the luggage out.

"No. All hotel vehicles are unavailable. Some insurance issue. Bound to be sorted out very quickly."

Audrey's eyes widened.

"So, you might as well answer my questions, Mrs Sutton," Pat said.

Col uttered an unpleasant word. "Audrey, give me a moment or two. I'll get my personal car and take you down there." He strode away.

"The keys, Cherry." Mandy hadn't moved.

With a similar word to the one her husband used, Cherry took a set of keys from her pocket and threw them on the ground.

Pat scooped them up and handed them to Mandy with a quiet, "Thank you."

Someone has to do something. We can't let Col leave with her.

"I noticed your beautiful diamond earrings the other night," Daphne said. "Pity about them."

"Pity about what?"

"How you lost one of the diamonds."

"I most certainly did not!"

"Oh, but we found the missing piece. That's what Pat was going to speak to you about. If you can identify it then he doesn't have to process it through the station."

Pat disguised the flash of surprise by making his face even sterner than usual, and most importantly, he said nothing although his eyes widened.

"Where did you find it?"

"In the garden. John has very good eyesight and he saw a glint and there it was. A diamond. Luckily, I remembered seeing there was one missing from yours. At least, I think it matches. Or maybe you are better just to take it to the station, Constable Patterson."

"May I see it at least?" Audrey finally stepped away from the car door.

Pat took the plastic bag out and handed it to her.

"Well... it does look like mine. And they have great value to me. Sentimental and monetary wise. Thank you!" She curled her fingers around the bag.

"I can't leave it with you until sighting the earring itself to make sure it belongs in it," Pat said.

"Fine. Then, can I go?" Audrey didn't wait for an answer but moved to the back of the vehicle. "Cherry, please get my largest bag down."

"You shouldn't." Cherry didn't move.

"Let me." John reached in and pulled out a suitcase. "This one?" He lay it down on the driveway.

"Yes. I'd like some privacy while I open it, please. Wouldn't want you to have a shock at my lingerie. If it fell out." She raised an eyebrow and John nodded and wandered away. Audrey unzipped the suitcase and raised the top.

From the far side of the building, where the garage was, a jeep turned the corner.

Heart racing, Daphne edged to where she could see the contents of the suitcase. Once Col got here the chance might disappear.

Audrey dug around, moving clothes to find a jewellery box.

"Here it is." She dropped the top but not before Daphne saw what she'd hoped for. If she could have fist pumped the air, she would have.

After opening her jewellery box, Audrey lifted one of the earrings she'd worn twice around Daphne. "There is a stone missing. How odd."

"So, you didn't notice this?"

"Well, no. It was there on Friday night. And Saturday."

"Negatory. I noticed the diamond was gone during the lunch break. When you were tearing into Stacy. And me. I almost said something to you then, but you were so intent on being angry that it slipped my mind."

Col stopped a few metres away, the motor running, and stepped out. Cherry rushed over and spoke to him. It was a brief, intense conversation which ended with them moving to stand on either side of the jeep.

Audrey turned and looked at them, her head tilted. Then she glanced back at Daphne.

"I'm going to leave now. May I take the diamond, constable?" She added the bag to the jewellery box and replaced the earring before closing the box. "If you need to speak to me about Darren, you have my contact details already. Col. Cherry. Please transfer my luggage."

As she leaned down to put her jewellery box in her suitcase, Col took a couple of steps forward, his eyes on Pat. Then he stopped again and glanced back at his wife.

"How did you get the laptop, Audrey?" Daphne asked.

Audrey straightened, her suitcase still unzipped. "Okay, I'm done with this interrogation. You are a common woman, Daphne.

Not a police officer or even a private detective. A busybody of the highest order is all you are."

"But Constable Patterson is a police officer. Pat, I just saw that laptop bag in her suitcase. The same one I saw in the suite reserved for Darren."

The other woman's mouth formed an 'O'.

Mandy, who'd stayed back the whole time, nodded. "The head housekeeper confirmed the laptop bag was in Mr Sutton's room on Saturday morning when she went in to check the window. We've had reports of leaks around a few windows and have been progressively improving the seals."

"For goodness' sake, this is my laptop. I have two and don't know what you are driving at. When I still expected Darren to arrive, I'd been working in his suite. The balcony has a nicer view than mine. I left it there and then picked it up again once he said he wasn't going to be here," Audrey snapped.

"When did he tell you he wasn't joining you here?" Pat asked.

"Late. I don't know. Col waited at the carpark and he didn't show. I rang him. Or he rang. I can't remember."

"If I search your luggage, I will only find one laptop, then?" Pat asked.

"You have no right to touch my things."

Daphne couldn't help herself. "Have you been up to the fountain recently?"

If looks could kill, Daphne would at the least need an ambulance after the glare from Audrey.

"I haven't been there at all this visit."

"You're certain?" Pat asked in a very even tone.

"You are just as stupid as she is. I said I hadn't been to the fountain or even to that garden on this trip."

"Audrey." Cherry hissed from near the jeep. She was tapping her ear and her head kept making sharp little gestures in the general direction of the path to the English garden.

"What have you done, Audrey?"

Rupert's voice boomed from above and everybody looked up.

He was on his balcony, hands on the balustrade and disbelief all over his face.

"Are you responsible for Darren's death? Are you?"

She shrank at the fury in his voice, her eyes darting to Pat, then Daphne, then Col.

"N... no. He died in a car accident."

Pat shook his head. "He died elsewhere and was placed into his car some hours before being found."

Audrey laughed.

Getting hysterical, dear, now the truth is coming out?

"None of this is funny. None of it." Rupert went inside.

"What *is* funny is how you think it remotely possible I had anything to do with my husband's death. I do wish you would explain to me how I managed to get down to the river, kill my husband, somehow get him into his car, then be back here before anyone noticed me missing?" Audrey gestured to her body. "I'm petite. Darren is twice my size. Not physically possible and besides, I was never on my own for the whole of Saturday." She folded her arms with a satisfied smile.

"I'll explain it," Daphne said. She wasn't about to lose this hard-won momentum. Over at the jeep, Col and Cherry had their doors open but were listening. Waiting.

Her legs shook so she braced them further apart. John was too far away for her to feel his encouraging touch, but he smiled at her and she drew in a quick breath.

"I believe Darren did arrive at the hotel. Most people were at dinner and most of the reception staff were on their break to take advantage of the quiet time. Darren either came through a back entrance or someone was at the desk who wouldn't say anything."

"Cherry!" Mandy burst out. "Cherry told me I was needed somewhere and she'd watch the front. I was only gone ten minutes."

"Liar." Cherry put a foot into the jeep.

Pat finally seemed to notice the movement around the jeep. He took his phone out and tapped a message.

Rupert strode from the hotel, carrying his red velvet jacket in one hand as Daphne continued.

"For some reason he didn't join Audrey on the roof or make his presence felt. And then later, when almost everyone was asleep, he went to the English garden. Something must have encouraged him to go there after midnight. I heard he didn't sleep well so perhaps he went for a walk. But when he got there, he was murdered."

"Don't look at me!" Audrey said. "I was asleep in bed."

"Stop pretending, Audrey." Rupert held the jacket higher. "This jacket has been a source of many hours of entertainment between Darren and I, and for those who don't understand, it was his originally. I won it from him in a game of poker. He won it back playing blackjack. And so on for years. And I deliberately wore it on Friday night expecting him to turn up and we'd end up gambling over it again. And you knew, Audrey, that although we laughed about it, Darren really wanted it back to keep."

Another piece of the puzzle.

"I wonder if Audrey told him she had the jacket and to meet her at the fountain. Nice and dark and secluded up there," Daphne pondered aloud. "Perhaps with a bottle of champagne to toast the moment, because Col found a full bottle there and Stacy hadn't got one left to take."

Rupert clasped the jacket against his torso. His eyes were bright with unshed tears.

"There was no reason for Stacy to harm Rupert. But you, Audrey? You wanted to buy this hotel and needed Darren's shares to do so. Putting a handful of magnets in the inside top pocket knowing he'd put the jacket on was easy. It didn't require physical strength. Just a bit of deception."

"None of this is true. How would I even have moved his body?" The conviction was gone from Audrey's voice, leaving a waver.

The roar of the jeep's motor startled them all. Col and Cherry were in it as it hurtled past them, wheels on the grass and pebbles flying everywhere as it tore toward the exit.

Pat shaded his eyes to watch its progress.

"Shouldn't we go after it?" John asked.

"Give it a minute."

The jeep had almost reached the gate when the flashing blue and red lights of a 4WD police vehicle blocked their way.

"Please continue, Daphne." Pat grinned.

"It was them! It was *all* their doing. They arranged to get Darren and keep him busy until late. They put the magnets in the jacket. They killed my husband then put his body into Cherry's 4WD. And she drove down early in the morning once the gate was unlocked and put him into his car and pushed it into the river. I never went near any of it."

"Then why, Audrey, did my husband and this constable fish *your* diamond from *your* earring out of the fountain?"

"I am so proud of you." John settled into a chair beside Daphne and opposite Rupert around a table in the foyer. "You had all the pieces and put them together."

"Not quite all. Rupert's information about the jacket made a big difference."

Rupert had said little since the arrest of Audrey, Col, and Cherry. He'd given his beloved jacket to Pat, who'd promised to return it to him promptly, but whether Rupert really wanted it back was the question. He'd muttered something about it being a death jacket.

Once Audrey had heard where they'd found her diamond, she gave up. She admitted to having been present at the fountain but claimed all she'd done was ask Darren to go for a walk to ask if he'd decided about the shares. When he'd said he intended to retire, not invest in the hotel, Col and Cherry had taken over. Their original plan, if his answer was not to their liking, was to overpower Darren and hold the magnets against his chest to make it look as though his pacemaker failed. The discovery of the red jacket on the roof had made it much easier as he'd put it on himself and succumbed too quickly to do more than cry out once.

She'd been quick to blame the others, explaining that Col had access to every room and easily planted the magnets in Stacy's suitcase after they'd accidentally left the one in his jacket found by housekeeping. "He even found her key to the awards box and put that death threat in there." Audrey had then demanded a lawyer.

"What about Stacy?" Daphne asked.

"I believe she'll be brought back a little later today. Pat apparently spoke to Leon and they aren't pressing charges against her."

"But everything will change," Rupert said. There was a deep sadness and weariness about the man. "She can't keep her position. Not after so many scandals. And I'm not sure who could take over who would be as passionate about the association as she was."

"Jessica," Daphne suggested. "She asks a lot of questions, and her ethics are cast in stone."

"Hmm. Worth considering. I guess you aren't interested, buttercup?"

Daphne took John's hand. "I've worked all my life and now I intend to spend the rest of my days enjoying time with my husband, our caravan, friends, and our family. Being a celebrant is a wonderful add on, but if I need to give something up, it is officiating."

"You won't have to do that for a long time, Daph," John said.

"Rupert? I'm happy to help the association from time to time. I'm happy to help you find a replacement. And I'm happy to call you my friend."

"But?" Rupert smiled as if he already knew what she'd say.

"No more buttercup."

The three of them laughed until Mandy arrived with a tray. She smiled at each one as she placed iced tea onto coasters and a plate of cupcakes in the middle of the table.

"I am so grateful to you, Daphne. And John," she said.

"What will happen now? You've lost two staff members," Daphne asked.

"No. I've lost dead weight. In fact, I've gained a lot because those two were undermining me at every turn. The rest of the staff are so happy, and I am terribly sorry because I hadn't seen how this was affecting them."

"Will the owners still want to sell? I have a client who is always on the lookout for a special property. One which would be an investment," John said.

"I imagine so. And I'm hopeful I might keep my job after all."

"May I have the owner's details?"

Mandy's smile lit up the room. "You are too kind, Mr Jones. And you, Mrs Jones? You are welcome here any time you want, and I'll make sure you always get the best of our suites."

"Oi. If you mean my suite then think again." Rupert grinned.

"I do and there's nothing to think about."

The smile didn't leave her face as she almost danced across the foyer floor.

Rupert picked up the plate and offered it to Daphne to select from. "No calling you buttercup. How about cupcake?"

Daphne stood at the balcony. The humidity and the threat of a storm was gone after a refreshing and unexpected rainfall while they had their massages. Her shoulders were relaxed, if slightly painful, thanks to Maisie's vigorous attention to their tenseness. But her back. Oh my. So amazing. Hot rocks were quite fantastic. Even John, who had been hesitant when they arrived at the day spa, had been glowing in his assessment of the massage.

The property was quiet. There were still police up at the English garden and the guests who remained were either in the pool or playing tennis, or else on the roof.

She loved it here. Despite the terrible events and feeling utterly exhausted, she loved the place. If only things had played out differently. No murderous wives. No evil employees.

"There you are. I got lost on my laptop for a bit, adding some of my river photos to Bluebell's Blessings and when I looked up, you'd gone." John put his arms around her, looking over her shoulder.

"Such a beautiful place. I hope my old client buys it and leaves Mandy in charge. We'll come back often."

"I'd like that."

John's presence helped. But she still had questions and still couldn't fathom why anyone would murder their own spouse. She might be good at piecing puzzles together but understanding motives was too hard. Poor Darren.

"We haven't packed yet. I need to get started."

John's arms tightened. "You've done a good thing."

"And I would really, really like to go soon."

"Me too. So, let's go and pack."

Bluebell was probably the best thing Daphne had ever seen. The carpark only had a couple of cars left, including a bright yellow Mustang with the plates 'RUPERTS'.

John did his customary check of the outside and backed the car to hook up Bluebell. Daphne made certain there was nothing loose inside. She'd unpack when they got home. For they were heading home, to Rivers End. They'd stop that night to have a decent sleep but by this time tomorrow she'd walk into their house. Open their curtains. And be home.

She picked up the one remaining item which needed securing in a cupboard. The snow globe of Rivers End. For a moment she played with it, turning it upside down and watching snowflakes fall upon the town which never had snow. A treasured gift from a treasured friend.

"Ready, Daph?" John stuck his head through the open door. "We can leave whenever you want."

"That would be now, love." She popped the snow globe into an overhead cupboard. "Let's go home."

A LETTER FROM THE AUTHOR

Huge thanks for reading *Of Retreats and Revenge*. I hope you loved this further instalment in Daphne's sleuthing adventures. If you want to join other readers in hearing all about my new releases and bonus content, you can sign up for my newsletter.

www.stormpublishing.co/phillipa-nefri-clark

If you enjoyed this book and could spare a few moments to leave a review, that would be hugely appreciated. Even a short review can make all the difference in encouraging a reader to discover my books for the first time. Thank you so much.

Daphne and John Jones appeared in my very first book and continued through that series as minor characters. Daphne's kindness and willingness to jump into any situation to offer a helping hand made her a popular part of those stories. And her cookies, of course. Out of the blue, Daphne announced she'd become a wedding celebrant and at that point, I knew she deserved her own series.

I'm a big fan of later-in-life adventures so the addition of a cute caravan named Bluebell and a new career as a travelling celebrant was perfect for Daphne. And while officiating weddings and funerals brings its own drama, throwing in a murder or two gave Daphne a chance to unleash her inner sleuth! Even John warmed up to the idea of solving crimes along with his own plans to make Daphne's life even happier.

Thanks again for being part of this amazing journey with me

and I hope you'll stay in touch—I have so many more stories and ideas to entertain you with! From my heart to yours.

Phillipa

www.phillipaclark.com

facebook.com/PhillipaNefriClark
instagram.com/phillipanefriclark
tiktok.com/@PhillipaNefriClark

www.ingramcontent.com/pod-product-compliance
Lightning Source LLC
Chambersburg PA
CBHW011559190726
48287CB00010B/2963